# Tell me What you See

## Zoran DRVENKAR

Translated from the German
by Chantal Wright

The Chicken House
2, Palmer Street, Frome, Somerset BA11 1DS

**From the Chicken House**

Here's a Gothic chiller – with a heart, and a very
unexpected soul – by a brilliant new writer. It's about the
supernatural and the possessed, but also the real, the
heartfelt and the *gift* inside each and every one of us.
Perhaps it's also about true friendship and goodness – but
you decide!

Barry Cunningham
Publisher

*tell me what you see*
*yeah tell me what you see*
*i'm caught beneath your heel, babe*
*an it's you that must let go*
Mojave 3

Copyright text © 2002 by Carlsen Verlag GmbH, Hamburg
First published in Germany under the title Sag Mir Was Du Siehst
All rights reserved
English translation copyright © Chantal Wright 2005

First published in Great Britain in 2005
The Chicken House
2 Palmer Street
Frome, Somerset BA11 1DS
United Kingdom
www.doublecluck.com

Cover design by Ian Butterworth
Cover illustration by Jo Hassall
Designed and typeset by Dorchester Typesetting Group Ltd
Printed in Great Britain

1 3 5 7 9 10 8 6 4 2

British Library Cataloguing in Publication data available.
Library of Congress Cataloging in Publication Data available.

ISBN 1 904442 55 2

The events of this novel take place in the western part of the city of Berlin, and follow the flow of the River Havel as it passes along the city's western edge, through several lakes to the wooded banks of the Grosser Wannsee.

# Part 1

# Alissa The Winter Child

It's dark outside, and I'm standing by the window cursing the winter. I can still remember how much I wished it would snow at Christmas when I was a child. I wanted to see thick flakes of snow falling from the sky and ice crystals on the windows. On the nights leading up to Christmas I would lie in bed impatiently, staring out into the darkness. Although I wished for it from the very bottom of my heart, it never snowed at Christmas. Not once. And now today's weather is taking its revenge on all those Christmases without snow.

Houses, cars and street lamps disappear behind a whirling white curtain. I can't see the pavement or the road. All I can see are the eerie shadows of the treetops. They move their branches as though they're arms waving up from the bottom of the sea.

It's six o'clock on Christmas Day. A fairytale winter scene stretches out in front of me and I'm cursing it as best I can.

'Shit!' I say. 'It's never going to stop.'

'If it doesn't stop, we'll do it some other time,' says Evelin.

She makes it sound like a question.

I don't say anything. I press my forehead against the glass and close my eyes. For a moment the snow isn't real, for a moment there's no reason to stay at home. I can hear Evelin's breathing in my ear. Of course we could do it some other time.

'It might stop soon.' My best friend is trying to calm me down.

I open my eyes again.

'I don't think so.'

Evelin sighs loudly.

'You don't have to come,' I say. 'It's OK if you—'

'I've been every year for the past three years,' she interrupts, 'no matter what the weather.'

'I know.'

'So?'

'So?'

'Will you pick me up?'

'I'll pick you up.'

Silence. Evelin's waiting for me to say goodbye. I'm waiting for her to change her mind.

'I'm not changing my mind,' says Evelin.

'Right. I'll see you later then,' I say, and hang up.


It was hardest keeping my eyes open just before midnight. I was tired of eating and talking. I was also tired of my little brother. I love him very much, but he'd been getting on my nerves for the previous two hours. Nobody wanted to play with him; nobody wanted to try out his new toys.

'Go to Alissa,' my mother kept saying.

Me of all people. Thanks very much. I'd been thinking about nothing but the weather all day, but that's over now. I'm lying in bed, listening to the snow falling against my window, and I'm calm inside. The sound makes me sleepy. It's like a cat touching the window with its nose. I rub my eyes and yawn. The clock says four minutes past one. There are no more voices in the living room, and there's no light from the hallway falling through the cracks around my door.

Christmas is over.

I swing my legs out of bed and get dressed. I put a torch, a box of matches and candles in my coat pockets. I tiptoe out of my room, along the hallway and out of the flat with my boots in my hand. I only stop holding my breath when the door has quietly clicked shut behind me. If my mother knew what I was doing, she'd be after me like a shot. And if my stepfather knew, he'd be right behind her trying to prevent the worst.

I sit down on the top step in the stairway and fasten my bootlaces in the dark. Then I wrap my scarf more tightly around my neck and put on my gloves. Without turning on the stair light, I run down the two flights of steps and out on to the street.

I'm alone. There are no people, no cars, no tracks on the white carpet of snow. The air is bitterly clear, the snow crunches under my boots. I look up at the sky. Flakes of snow spin towards me as though they have travelled thousands of miles just to say hello. I pull my hat down so that it covers my ears and cross the road.

My father died six and a half years ago crossing a road.

It was one of those rainy summer days that you welcome because they make the heat bearable for a couple of hours. I was nine years old at the time and I was sitting with my parents in a café. We were just about to leave for a holiday in Holland. Everything was packed and there was only an hour to go before we were due to leave when suddenly the rain came pelting down. We were sitting in a café eating cakes and drinking hot chocolate, feeling glad that it had cooled off a bit, when my mother saw Uncle Lucas on the other side of the street. Uncle Lucas was my father's brother. He was standing in the pouring rain reading the bus timetable. My father wanted to bring him over to join us in the café. He ran out into the rain and called his brother's name. I remember Uncle Lucas turning around and looking surprised. And I still remember my father waving at him and hunching his shoulders before he crossed the road. Then a lorry came and I saw everything.

For a while I felt as though I'd lost my father completely. That was a long time ago. Now I know that he's always with me. Nothing can erase him from my memory. And that's why I'm cursing the winter tonight and fighting my way through this snow. It isn't easy sharing your life with a dead person. But it's a lot better than forgetting somebody and carrying on with your own life as though there's just been a commercial break and nothing much else has happened.

Evelin lives ten minutes away from me in a house that used to belong to her great-grandparents. There's a phone box at the end of the street. I have to force open the door because of all the snow that's piled up in front of it. My fingers are so cold that I can barely hold the phone card. Evelin picks up after the sixth ring.

'Oh God!' she says.

'What's the matter?'

'I put the phone under my pillow, so it wouldn't wake anybody up and when it rang it nearly scared me to death. It was like one of those dreams where somebody calls you and then you can't find the phone.'

'How frightening,' I say, rolling my eyes.

'Where are you then?' asks Evelin.

'About eleven houses down.'

Evelin yawns. I can hear her getting out of bed.

'What's the weather like?' she asks.

I rub the steam off the phone box window and look outside. I can just about make out the other side of the street through the heavy snowfall.

'It's almost stopped snowing,' I say.

\*    \*    \*

We make our way down *Kastanienallee*. We can't tell if we're still walking on the pavement or have stepped on to the road. The houses around us look as though they're asleep. Here and there you can see the glow of colourful fairy lights or the blue flicker of a television breaking on the whiteness of the snow. Most of the windows are dark. The few lights we can see look on like watchful eyes. Christmas is definitely over.

Evelin's face is hidden behind a scarf. She's pulled her woolly hat down so far that only her eyes are visible. Neither of us talks very much. Whenever I open my mouth, the wind blows snow crystals into my throat. They feel like powdered glass. And whenever Evelin speaks, it sounds as though she's chewing cotton wool.

'It *has* almost stopped snowing, hasn't it?' she says for at least the tenth time.

'There's only a bit of snow,' I say.

'If only I'd known,' she adds.

'Then what?' I ask.

Evelin thinks it through for a minute. Then she laughs and says, 'I don't know.'

On *Spandauer Damm* we can see that the first snow-ploughs have been and gone already. Piles of snow form ramparts along both sides of the street.

The cars parked next to them form little hills. There's no traffic and the traffic lights are on red.

'You're not going to wait for the green man,' says Evelin

firmly, tugging at my arm. We cross the road, run into *Königin Elisabeth Strasse* and turn left into a side street a hundred metres further on. We leave the pale light of the street lamps behind us and stop in front of a fence. Evelin looks at me.

'You owe me one after this, OK?'

'Yeah.'

We've had practice climbing this fence. Almost simultaneously we dig our fingers into the holes in the wire and are on the other side within a minute. Evelin's hat has slipped. I straighten it and push a strand of her hair back underneath. As we watch our tracks being covered by the falling snow, the wind dies down for a minute. The snowflakes fall thick and heavy.

'OK?' I ask, getting out the torch.

'OK,' says Evelin.


Out on the streets the night was bright and white. Here under the tall pine trees it's dark and blue. The treetops rustle and occasionally the rush of wet cars can be heard from the nearby motorway.

'I don't know,' says Evelin after a couple of metres. She stops walking and looks down at her boots which have sunk into the snow.

'What's the matter?'

'It doesn't feel right, walking over dead people like this, do you know what I mean?'

I feel exactly the same. The gravel paths that run between the rows of graves have disappeared and the wind has blown the snow zigzag into waist-high barricades. A few gravestones and crosses loom out of the darkness. Even though I've been here countless times, I've lost my sense of direction. I could do with the water fountain or the rubbish bins that tell me where to turn left. I could do with a bit less snow.

Evelin reads my thoughts.

'Don't tell me you don't know where we are.'

'Maybe. Do you recognize anything?'

She shakes her head.

'If you ask me, this isn't going to work!'

I don't ask her and move the torch beam over the snow. I know we'll manage. I promised my dad I would come tonight. I keep my promises.

After a few steps I notice that Evelin isn't following me. I stop walking and turn around.

'What's the matter?' I ask.

'Alissa, we can't just run around aimlessly, scraping the snow off every gravestone we see. You realize that, don't you?'

'That won't be necessary,' I say. 'It's not the first time we've been here.'

Evelin inclines her head and looks at me sceptically. I know what she's thinking. She's thinking that an upright gravestone wouldn't be such a problem. We would definitely see one of those. But the stone that my mum had made for my dad is embedded in the ground. We'll be lucky if we manage to fall over it.

'Let's find the mausoleum,' I say. 'Once we've found the mausoleum we'll find his grave.'

As I say it, the wind suddenly stops howling and it becomes very quiet. I point my torch at the sky. It's stopped snowing. A few flakes of snow are still making their way slowly down. They look as though they're twisting around the beam of the torch.

'Isn't that pretty?' I say.

'Pretty stupid,' says Evelin, taking the torch away from me.

## 2

# Evelin The Best Friend

'Sometimes I have no idea what's going on in your head,' I say.

'Not much,' answers Alissa.

'Well, that's good to know,' I say, shining the torch over the cemetery.

I don't know why Alissa's mood swings still surprise me. I often imagine her colliding with a switch and flipping it by accident. From normal *click* to deep sadness *click* and back to normal. It's particularly bad on Christmas Day. I spend the whole day trudging round with my parents visiting relatives. Every year Alissa waits for me impatiently so that we can go and visit the cemetery. It doesn't matter what the weather's like. And now we're here, trying to remember where everything was before all this snow fell on Berlin. Things couldn't possibly be any worse.

'I think the mausoleum's over there,' says Alissa, pointing over to the left.

I shine the torch in that direction, but I can only see shadows.

'If you say so,' I say.

'What else would it be?'

'The toilets maybe.'

'There aren't any toilets here. Come on.'

It is the mausoleum. A few small fir trees are planted around it. They stand there like motionless guards. Alissa stops about thirty metres away from the mausoleum and decides that this is where we should start looking.

'He must be somewhere around here,' she says.

'Somewhere around here,' I echo.

'You take the torch.'

'But you won't be able to see anything then.'

'I'll recognize it all right.'

Alissa points forward.

'You look in this row, I'll come from the left and we'll meet at the mausoleum, OK?'

I watch her until I can't see her any more in the darkness. She stops next to a pile of snow and kicks it. It makes a noise. She crouches down and starts scraping the snow off a gravestone with her hands. I hunch up my shoulders and get to work.

Her mother has no idea about our visits to the cemetery. If she knew where we were now she'd probably freak out. On her dad's birthday, Alissa and her mum come here together. At some point that wasn't enough for Alissa any more. It started in her first term at secondary school. She leaned over to me during a physics lesson and whispered:

'Do you know what day it is today?'

'A crappy day to be at school,' I said. It was hot, and I hoped they might send us home because of the heat.

'No,' said Alissa. 'My dad died two years ago today.'

I swallowed and squinted at her out of the corner of my eye.

'Really? Are you serious?' I asked.

'I'm serious. Will you come with me?'

'Come with you where?'

'Idiot!' said Alissa, turning to face the front of the class again.

Later she explained to me that the anniversary of her dad's death was much more important to her than his birthday.

'I was there,' she said. 'It's an important day for both of us.'

The anniversary of his death *and* Christmas.

When I asked her what was so special about Christmas, Alissa looked at me as though I needed my head examining and said, 'The cold, of course.'

Of course. I could have thought of that myself.

I never asked a question like that again.


'And?'

'Nothing!' I call out into the darkness.

My hands are wet and frozen in their gloves. The torch has already slipped out of my fingers a couple of times. The last time it gave a flicker and wouldn't work any more. I've scraped off about ten thousand gravestones. I'm sweating like somebody sitting in a sauna wearing a coat and a woolly hat. When I look up, the dark shadow of the mausoleum looms out directly in front of me. Alissa joins me two minutes later.

'I could have sworn he was further to the left,' she says.

'My fingers are frozen,' I say, taking off my gloves and putting them into my coat. It's only then that I realize she took her gloves off a long time ago. She grabs hold of my hands and rubs them between hers.

'Built-in central heating,' she says, and I can feel how hot her fingers are.

It didn't use to be like that. A year after her dad died, Alissa began to freeze. It was the middle of summer. The doctors were mystified and talked about a virus. They said it would soon pass. But it didn't – it got worse. Her whole body was frozen. She felt as though winter had moved in. But she didn't talk to anybody about it. I was the only one she told.

'There aren't many places left,' I say, looking back at what we've uncovered.

There's a small patch remaining between those paths that Alissa and I have already searched. Despite the bright snow, the area is difficult to make out in the darkness. There could be ten graves or so hidden underneath it.

'We'll find him,' I say, to cheer Alissa up.

She looks at the patch, as though a gust of wind might free her dad's grave from the snow at any minute. I can tell from the shadows under her eyes that she hasn't slept much over the past few nights. But that has nothing to do with

Christmas. The problem is Simon.

'I could sleep over at your place,' I say.

'Tonight?'

'Why not?'

'But your parents . . .'

'. . . will find a note in the kitchen explaining everything.'

Alissa looks at me in surprise.

'You left them a note?'

'Of course,' I say, picturing my dad's face – he's the first person in the kitchen in the morning – when he finds the note stuck to the fridge. I know he'll understand. We're past discussions and punishments. He and my mum only want to know where I am, that's all.

'You and your forward thinking!' says Alissa, laughing. 'And how do I explain to Sarah and Robert that you just happened to finish up in my bed on Christmas Day?'

'If anybody even asks,' I say.

'They'll definitely think I'm a lesbian.'

I have to laugh.

'Robert would never think that.'

'Robert wouldn't, but Sarah would.'

'Rubbish!' I say.

'Yeah, yeah,' says Alissa, avoiding my gaze.

She doesn't get on with her mum. Sometimes I even think she likes her stepfather better. He's a really quiet type, one of those people who keep the peace. Takes all the blame and smiles.

'Are you warm again?' asks Alissa, letting go of my hands.

'Much better,' I say. I can feel a pleasant tingling in my fingertips.

Alissa tries the torch one last time, then puts it in her coat pocket and says, 'We can manage without it.'

'Maybe we should stick together,' I suggest. 'What do you think? It'd be stupid to lose each other out here.'

We both look up at the sky at the same time. It's like a sheet of black glass. If the moon would only come out from behind the clouds, things would be much easier.

'OK,' says Alissa. 'Let's keep looking.'

We still can't find the grave.

'I don't believe it!' says Alissa, frustrated. She stops moving, her hands in her coat pockets, her shoulders hunched against the freezing cold and a strained expression around her mouth.

'I just don't believe it,' she says again.

We've searched the whole of the remaining patch piece by piece. Alissa didn't recognize any of the names. Her switch has flipped again. I can see that she's about to sink into a swamp of sadness.

'Let's look on the other side of the mausoleum,' I say, although it's the last thing I feel like doing.

Alissa looks at the gravestones we've uncovered and nods. I let out a sigh of relief. Anything's better than standing around not knowing what to do next. We go up to the mausoleum side by side. Occasionally our arms brush against each other, once I trip and almost fall over. As we pass the mausoleum, I catch the smell of flowers for a moment.

'Did you smell that?' I ask.

Alissa shakes her head. Her thoughts seem to be elsewhere.

'I can't believe the torch is broken,' she says, kicking angrily at a pile of snow.

'Do you know what I think?' I ask.

Alissa laughs and says, 'That this is the last time you're coming out here with me?'

'No, silly cow. I think that after a whole hour you could at least say something about Simon. Just one little sentence.'

No reply from Alissa. Typical.

'I mean, I don't want to fire questions at you,' I continue. 'I'd much prefer it if you'd just talk off your own bat.'

Still no answer.

'Sorry,' I say and stop walking. If I've made her cry, then I'm a real bitch.

I turn back towards her and then look all around me.

Alissa has disappeared.

3

# Alissa The Winter Child

I want to shout out my father's name. Or sit down in the snow and start crying with frustration. I don't know what Evelin would do then. She probably wouldn't laugh. But I don't shout and I don't cry. I look out over the cemetery as though none of it bothers me. My dad's grave has vanished and I hate Christmas more than anything else in the world.

'Let's look on the other side of the mausoleum,' says Evelin.

I can't think of anything better, so I nod and we make our way over. The snow sticks to my boots in clumps, weighing them down. Every step is an effort. I can see us messing around here till dawn. We've probably already walked over the stupid gravestone ten times without noticing. As soon as it's spring, I'm going to plant a fir tree right next to it. I'm not letting this happen again.

'Did you smell that?' asks Evelin.

I shake my head. The only thing I can smell is the night air. It's icy and cuts like a knife. If only we had some sort of light,

I'm sure we'd find the grave more quickly.

'I can't believe the torch is broken,' I say, kicking at the snow.

'Do you know what I think?' Evelin asks.

I laugh.

'That this is the last time you're coming out here with me?'

'No, silly cow. I think that after a whole hour you could at least say something—'

I don't hear any more. My legs disappear from underneath me and my stomach rises. The very next moment I land on something hard. My teeth bang together. Pain shoots like an electric shock from my head down to my feet. Then I lie still.

'Alissa?'

It's pitch black. I try to get up, but bright stars are dancing in front of my eyes.

'Alissa?'

Evelin's voice sounds muffled, an echoing whisper surrounding me on all sides. I lift my head. I can see a piece of sky through the blanket of snow above me.

'Here!' I call.

'Here!' I call again and the croak in my voice disappears.

Evelin's face appears in the crack. Some snow falls down.

'Oh shit!' she says.

I stand and stretch my arms up towards her. The crack is too far away. I reckon there must be at least three metres between me and Evelin.

'Alissa?'

'I'm down here,' I say.

Evelin moves her head.

'I can't see you.'

I strike a match and my eyes are dazzled by the light.

'Are you OK?'

'I'm OK,' I answer. 'You can throw the rope ladder down now.'

Evelin laughs, but then her laugh dies away and I can see the frightened expression on her face.

'What's it like down there?'

I light another match and hold it up in the air. Slowly, I turn around in a circle.

'It's some kind of underground vault. Try and see if the entrance to the mausoleum is open. Maybe there are some steps that lead down here. If not . . .'

'. . . I'll fetch my dad.' Evelin finishes my sentence for me.

I fall silent. The match goes out. Her dad is all right. Even though we both know there'll be trouble, her dad is still the best choice.

'See if you can find the entrance first, OK?'

'Right. And don't you go anywhere.'

I have to laugh, although I don't really feel like it.

Evelin's face disappears. I'm on my own.


*Don't you go anywhere* is easily said. Within seconds I'm looking for the exit. The room I've fallen into is a circular vault. There are three corridors leading out of it. I cup one hand protectively around the match, take the path on the left and enter a vault with niches in the wall. There are urns in the niches, and each urn has a metal plaque. I read the names and dates of the deceased. The oldest urn is from 1873, the most recent from 1988. I run my fingers over the delicate curve of the numbers before investigating further.

Only after the ninth match goes out does it occur to me to light one of the candles I've brought to put on my father's grave. I take it out of my coat pocket and hold the flame to the wick. The flame throws out a red light through the plastic cover, and even though it makes the shadows around me suddenly look threatening, I feel safer.

The vault with the urns doesn't lead anywhere. I go back and take the next path. It's unbelievably quiet down here. The noise my boots make reminds me of pebbles crunching against each other. I stand still for a moment and strain to hear Evelin.

'Hello!' I say.

*Hellohellohello!* replies the echo.

At the end of the second corridor the path curves and a few steps lead downwards. A high vault opens before me. I look up and see a mosaic ceiling. The small discs glow in various colours and reflect the candlelight. It's as though I'm shining a light into the eyes of a cat. It looks beautiful, almost like a painting. I hold the candle out in front of me. The red light follows my movements and enters the vault before me. It falls on a table in the centre of the room. At least I think it's a table. As I draw nearer, I can see that it's a stone plinth. No ornamentation, just smooth stone. And on the plinth lies a coffin.

I don't move. I stand stock still and look from the coffin back to my hand with the candle in it. My hand has begun to shake. I look back at the coffin and then back at my hand. It refuses to calm down.

'Shit!' I say, putting one hand around the other. That's better. The light from the candle stops flickering.

I look at the coffin again.

It's made of white varnished wood and is about as big as a guitar case. It must be a child's coffin. I feel myself starting to shake again. But it's not because I'm in the presence of a dead child.

No.

There's something else.

I go nearer, hold up the candle and immediately step back. I was right. There's a plant growing out of the light wood of the coffin lid. Its fine leaves stretch up towards the vault's mosaic ceiling.

# 4

# Evelin The Best Friend

Now I know where the smell comes from. There are flowers at the entrance to the mausoleum. Their scent lies sweet and heavy in the air, even though they're covered in snow. There are roses and carnations and fir tree branches, and in between them two small presents decorated with a ribbon.

I pull at the door. Locked. I shake the handle. Then I walk around the mausoleum. There are no windows. I stop in front of the hole that Alissa fell into and bend over it carefully. It wouldn't help if I fell in there too.

'Alissa?'

I wait for her to strike a match.

'Alissa?' I shout more loudly.

Still dark.

'Come on.'

Nothing.

'Great.'

I get up and start to run.

\* \* \*

A quarter of an hour later I'm standing in front of our house, gasping for breath. I unlock the door and I wait for my breathing to slow down, then I tiptoe into my parents' bedroom and stand on my dad's side of the bed. I don't know what to do next. I've never tried to wake up my dad with my mum lying next to him. One thing's certain: if my mum wakes up, then all hell will break loose.

I think of all the films I've seen where kidnappers hold their victims' mouths shut. The victims open their eyes and then the kidnappers hold their index fingers to their mouths and say *Shhhh!* The victims' eyes grow even wider and they nod.

I hope my dad has seen these films, and I put my hand gently over his mouth. The very next moment my mum sits bolt upright in bed and screams like crazy. The scream makes my father blink and look at me in surprise, then the scream dies away, the light on the other side of the bed goes on and my mum says, 'What the hell are you doing?'

I pull my hand back. I have no idea what to say to my mum. What I would most like to do is lie down next to them in bed for a bit. I'm completely exhausted from running. I slipped and fell twice on the way home. My arm hurts and I'm not in good shape. I'd love to just lie down.

'Hi, Evelin,' says my dad, sitting up.

'Hi,' I say, trying a smile.

'I have to talk to Dad,' I add, as though that explains everything.

'Why are you wearing your coat?' asks my mum.

'And why are you wearing your woolly hat?' asks my dad, bending over, probably to see if I'm wearing trousers and boots as well. I am wearing my trousers. I left my boots downstairs in the hallway.

'I've got a problem,' I say, sitting down on the edge of their bed.

Five minutes later I'm back on the street with my dad in tow. Mum wanted to drive us, but one look out of the window convinced her that it was a bad idea. Of course she wanted to come along as well, but my dad was against it. He knows that she'll suffer from lack of sleep in the morning. Mum has to leave at six to catch her train. She commutes to Hamburg three times a week from Berlin, even during the holidays. My dad thinks that's torture enough. There's no need for her to chase through the night to get my best friend out of a vault as well.

'Can't we go through the entrance?' asks my dad, gasping for breath, when we get to the fence.

'It's locked and two metres high,' I say, looking at him suspiciously. 'You can climb over a fence, can't you?'

He takes a good look at it.

'I'd prefer the entrance.'

'So?' I say.

'Show me how you do it,' he says.

I dig my hands in, swing myself over the top and land safely on the other side.

'Got it?'

He doesn't answer, but passes me a torch and a rope. Then he digs his hands in and almost tears half the fence down.

'Your leg!' I shout. 'Your leg!'

At last he manages to haul his leg over, pulls the other one over as well and lands with a muffled sound in the snow.

'Thanks,' he says, when I've helped him up. 'What now?'

I look around for a moment and find our footprints. Am I glad it's stopped snowing!

'Don't you think that Alissa's enthusiasm would be more healthily expressed during the daytime?' asks my father, following me.

'That's a nice way of putting it.'

'Seriously, Evelin, don't you think you could come out here during the day instead?'

'Dad, it's because of Christmas,' I say in an irritated voice. I've already explained this to him and my mum. 'I can only come here with Alissa at night, because every year at Christmas we have to visit all the relatives. That's the reason.'

My dad shuts up. I know he likes Alissa and I hope he's not getting a bad impression of her.

'Well, if you ask me,' he says finally, 'you don't have to come every year. Your mum and I can manage by ourselves.'

'You mean, no cousins and no aunts and uncles at Christmas?'

'As far as I'm concerned. I'd much prefer it if you came out here while it was still light.'

'We do that on the anniversary of his death.'

'That makes me feel much better.'

I point forward and speed up.

'That's the mausoleum. We have to be careful we don't fall through the same hole.'

The tracks cross over one another. It looks as though Alissa and I were dancing out here.

'Shall I go first?' I ask.

'You know your way around here better than I do,' answers my father. 'I'm only here to rescue your best friend from a hole.'

I know he's grinning. I look at him.

'Thanks again,' I say.

'Get on with it!' he says.

I light the way and try to find the hole with the beam from the lamp.

'Alissa?' I call out. 'Alissa!'

# Alissa The Winter Child

There's a narrow crack in the top right section of the coffin lid where the stalk has pushed its way through the wood. I put the candle down on the lid and look closely at the plant. It can't be any more than ten centimetres tall. It's purple, almost black. I can see fine hairs and veins on the leaves. The leaves quiver when I run my finger over them.

On one side of the coffin there are hinges, on the other side metal fastenings. I've seen similar fastenings on suitcases. There's no lock, only the fastenings. I take the candle off the lid and turn around to look more closely at the vault. I want to do something else to stop me from thinking about this coffin, but there's nothing else to see. The mosaic pattern on the roof is just about everything. No niches, no urns, no other exit that might lead to freedom.

Only the stone plinth and the coffin.

I walk round the coffin, counting the fastenings. The hot oily smell of the candle creeps into my nose. I ought to go back. Evelin's waiting for me. I shouldn't put the candle on top of the coffin lid again. I know that's the wrong thing to do. But my hands won't obey me any more. My fingers do as they please. I force them under my armpits and try to calm myself down.

I take a few steps towards the exit. I don't get very far. I stop and turn back to the coffin. My hands free themselves from my armpits and wander over the metal fastenings. It happens so quickly that the individual clicks sound like a single noise. I'm bathed in sweat, feverish. I put the candle down on the edge of the stone plinth and push up the lid of the coffin. I don't know what's wrong with me. That's not me. I'm not the one . . .

The plant is growing out of a dead child's chest.

It's a boy. His arms are lying by his sides. His face is pale, his lips are blue, his hair a light blonde. He's wearing trousers and a jacket. They make him look like a miniature adult. He can't be any older than five. Five years old and dead.

The jacket has slipped over to the left side of his chest. The plant has pushed through his shirt, moving the jacket to one side in order to force its way through the coffin lid. When I open the lid the stalk breaks off a couple of centimetres above the boy's chest.

I bend over the corpse, ignoring the smell, ignoring the face and the proximity of the dead body. I carefully place my thumb and index finger around the remainder of the stalk sticking out of the boy's chest, and pull.

It's deeply rooted, immovable.

I walk around the coffin to pull at the piece of the plant

stuck in the open lid. It slides out. I smell the plant and hold the leaves up in front of my eyes before putting it carefully inside my coat.

My head is humming as I do it. It's a melody that won't go away. No matter what I do, I can't get rid of it. I can't think straight.

Before I know what I'm doing, I've closed the lid and shut the fastenings. I take the candle, leave the vault and wander around. I only calm down when I see the hole over my head. And then I can think again. And I do think. But only nonsense. And then I look back.

*Was that me?*

*Did I just open the coffin?*

*Did I—*

I hear a noise and look up. A splinter of night sky looks down at me like a questioning eye.

*Hello!*

For a second I think somebody has called my name.

I listen.

I incline my head.

*Maybe somebody in the vault back there? Maybe the boy is coming and wants his plant back . . .*

I don't move. I listen and feel the sweat running into my eyes. Then I hear footsteps, hear the echo of footsteps in the vault. Behind me, next to me, above me, very close. I look up. At that very moment Evelin falls towards me.

# Evelin's Father

I wish I'd stayed in bed. I approach the hole cautiously. It's dark below.

'Evelin!' I call.

'Ouch!'

'Be careful!'

Alissa's voice *and* Evelin's. I'm relieved.

'Any broken bones?' I ask.

'I landed on top of her,' answers Evelin, and to my surprise I can hear the two of them laughing.

'How about throwing the rope up to me,' I call down.

'*You've* got the rope?' I hear Alissa say.

'Who else?' says Evelin, and they laugh again.

A match is struck. They've even got a candle down there.

'Is the torch OK?' I ask.

A moment later the beam of the torch hits me right in the face.

'Thanks,' I say.

'Catch!' says my daughter.

I stretch out my arm and catch the rope.

'OK, I've got it. I'm just going to find a good place to fasten it and then I'll pull you up.'

I fasten the end to the iron bars on the mausoleum and unfurl the rope until it reaches the hole.

'Damn! It's too short,' I say.

'What?'

'Oh no!'

'Just kidding,' I reassure them, throwing down the end of the rope.

Evelin is the first one to be pulled up. She didn't appreciate my joke at all.

'I nearly wet myself,' she said. 'That's a proper vault down there, you know.'

Alissa isn't upset about anything. She's just happy to be out of the hole. When I offer to have a quick look round to see if we can still find her dad's grave, her eyes light up.

The remaining snow-covered graves are clearly visible in the torchlight. The fourth one belongs to Alissa's father. I don't know how they could have missed it.

I draw back and leave the two girls alone. When they turn back towards me, they're holding hands. All that's left behind are two candles and a lot of tracks in the snow.

# Alissa The Winter Child

'Are you sure?'

'Absolutely,' I say, looking up at the brightly lit windows of her house.

Evelin waits. That's not a good enough answer.

'I'm just tired,' I lie, because even though I know it's warm and cosy in her house, I want to get away.

'But we could . . .'

Evelin trails off and continues a moment later. 'I'm just worried about you, you know? Because of Simon. You didn't want to talk about him—'

I hug her so tightly that she stops talking.

'OK, OK, that's enough,' she says, freeing herself from my grasp. 'I'll shut up now.'

'Thanks,' I say, buttoning up my coat. 'Do you fancy having breakfast at my place tomorrow?'

Evelin thinks that's a great idea and leans forward to give me a kiss on the cheek. It's painful to leave her behind.

'When you fell in there I was so worried about you,' she

says with a sudden, short, broken laugh.

'I'm going to go now,' I say, 'otherwise I'll start crying.'

I give Evelin one last hug and then I make my way down the steps to the street.

When I get to the phone box, I turn around. My best friend is still standing in the doorway. She looks as though she's been cut out of an ancient black and white film. I don't wave to her. I know if I wave now, I'll never go home. I'll run back and spend the night with her, and tell her what happened in the vault.

*If only I could!*

My arms hang stiffly at my sides. My fingers twitch, but nothing else moves. I don't know what's wrong with me.

The familiar smell of the flat surrounds me. Nobody has noticed that I've been outside half the night. I tiptoe into the bathroom.

Here, at home, I feel as though the world can't come in. These rooms are untouchable, these people are safe from everything that happens outside. My father would never have died here. It only got him on the street. Home is safe.

I lie in bed with this feeling and have no idea how I got there. This is what a time lapse must feel like. Just now I was in the bathroom and now I'm lying in bed trying to forget the night. I don't want to think. I shouldn't think. I'm so tired I just want to sleep and wake up in the morning with a clear head.

The window is slightly open. I can smell the cold air, the snow and the wind and the ice. Everything's fine. I've visited my dad's grave. I've kept my promise.

Sleep.

# Part II

# Elia and Aren

They enter through the half-open bathroom window and move silently along the hallway. They lift their heads and move them searchingly in all directions before coming to a stop in front of the last room. They go in, close the door and listen in the darkness.

*Something's not right.*

They can feel it.

*Something's wrong.*

The figure on the right places his hands on the wall and shakes his head. The figure on the left crouches down and moves his hand over the floor.

*Nothing here either.*

Confusion.

Then a noise.

They look at each other, then look at the bed. The girl is sitting up. Her hair fans out around her face, her skin has a pale shimmer, her eyes are dark caves. It looks as though she's woken from a nightmare. They can hear her heavy breathing.

*I feel as though she can see us.*

*Nonsense.*

The figure on the right looks around the room.

*We must have made a mistake. This isn't the right place.*

*But you can feel it . . .*

*Yes, I can feel it.*

The figure on the left touches his forehead with his hand. The figure on the right doesn't take his eyes off the girl.

*I'm telling you, she can see us.*

*Nonsense. She had a bad dream. Can't you hear how fast her heart is beating?*

*But her eyes are open . . .*

*She can dream with her eyes open too.*

'Who are you?' says the girl.

The two figures start back. Then they are calm again.

*I told you, she can see us.*

'Can you see us?' asks the figure on the left, coming closer.

'I'll scream,' warns the girl. You can tell that she means it.

With three quick steps the figure on the right reaches the bed and touches the girl on the arm.

'Keep calm . . .'

The girl calms down. She looks from one to the other, then leans over to one side and switches on the bedside lamp.

'That's better,' she says.

The figure on the left is a man with black shoulder-length hair. His long coat is open and underneath he's wearing a white T-shirt. The figure on the right is a head shorter. His body looks chunky and compact, probably because of the large jumper he's wearing instead of a coat. His hair is standing up wildly on his head, and he begins to stroke it into place as though he has just noticed.

'Who are you?' asks the girl.

The tall figure turns away from the bed.

*Let's go.*

*Why can she see us?*

*I don't know. Let's just go.*

*You know why she can see us.*

*No, I—*

'What are you looking for?' asks the girl.

'We're sorry we burst in on you like this,' explains the small figure, bowing briefly before turning away and following the tall figure to the door.

'I know what you're looking for,' says the girl.

The two men stop moving.

'It's the plant, isn't it? You came because of the plant. Am I right?'

The two men turn around slowly, and for the first time the girl feels afraid of them.

'Who are you?' she asks again and it takes all her courage not to jump out of bed.

'We won't get anywhere like this,' says the small one, walking around the bed. The tall one moves at the same time. It's like watching a perfectly choreographed ballet. The two men sit down left and right on the edge of the bed at the very same moment. The girl is between them and doesn't know which of the two she should look at.

'Elia,' says the small one.

'Aren,' says the tall one.

'Alissa,' says the girl, shaking hands with first one, then the other.

She tells them that she couldn't sleep, that she waited and didn't know what the matter was. So she lay in bed with her eyes wide open, impatient.

'Then the door opened and you came in.'

Alissa talks about the vault and the coffin. The words are liberating – they tumble out with an ease that she hadn't felt when she said goodbye to her friend.

'We're too late,' says Aren when she's finished speaking, and gets up from the bed. He stands at the window and looks out. The night sky has lost its dark blueness. The morning is approaching with every minute that goes by.

'I don't think it's too late,' says Elia, turning to Alissa. 'We need the plant, do you understand?'

'I . . . I didn't want to take it,' she explains, amazed that she can say this. She hadn't realized until this moment.

Elia shakes his head.

'That wasn't it. The plant wanted to be taken. Where is it?'

Alissa swings her legs out of bed. The clothes she was wearing during the night are lying over a chair. She pulls out her coat and reaches into the inside pocket.

Aren turns from the window. Elia has stood up and is waiting at the end of the bed.

*It's useless.*

*It's not.*

*But you can sense—*

'It must be here somewhere.'

Alissa turns each pocket inside out. Then she drops the
coat and searches through her jeans, checks under the chair
and rummages through her coat again, without finding the
plant.

'I . . .'

She looks up helplessly.

'Try and remember,' begs Elia.

'I . . . I came home and went straight to my room.'

'Did you go into the kitchen?' asks Elia. 'Did you take the
plant out of your coat pocket?'

'I . . . I don't think so.'

'You don't *think* so?'

'I don't know.'

Aren pushes himself away from the window and stops in
front of Alissa. He sniffs at her hair and then her throat
before looking at Elia.

*I told you, it's useless.*

*But she hasn't—*

*That's exactly what she's done.*

*No, that can't be! Not that fast.*

*Why do you think she can see us?*

*But so quickly . . .*

'What's the matter?' asks Alissa.

Now Elia is standing next to her as well and he too sniffs at Alissa as though she's an exotic flower. Finally he steps back and says quietly, 'I'm so sorry.'

'What?' asks Alissa. 'What's going on?'

Aren lifts his hands to quieten her down. Alissa has raised her voice without noticing.

'What's going on?' she says again quietly.

'The plant . . .'

Aren trails off. Elia says, 'It's not your fault, Alissa. It used you and we arrived too late. If anybody is to blame, then it's us.'

'What . . . what are you talking about? Why am I not to blame? I mean, to blame for what?' stammers Alissa. She touches her mouth and clutches at her throat, then her hands wander down to her stomach.

'We're sorry,' says Elia, taking a step back.

Alissa looks from him to Aren, then she runs out of the room. She doesn't care if she wakes up her mum, her brother or her stepfather. She storms down the hallway into the bathroom and just about manages to lift the toilet lid before she vomits.

# 9

# Alissa The Winter Child

Breathe.

I breathe with my eyes shut. My mouth opens and closes like a fish out of water that doesn't know what air is for. Just keep breathing. I only open my eyes after I've flushed the toilet twice.

My knees hurt. I get up and lower the toilet lid. I sit on the edge of the bath, waiting for the nausea to pass.

*It's not real. I've just woken up from a bad dream and it's not real. Mum will stick her head round the door any minute and ask me if I've eaten something dodgy. I'll hear Robert in the background talking to Jan, who's woken up. I think I can even hear his little voice asking 'Is Alissa OK? Is she ill?'*

I feel ill. I'm light-headed in a way that reminds me of rollercoaster rides. It's as though my head still has to come down and land on my neck. Weightless.

'Did you have a bad dream?'

My mother is standing in the doorway, looking sleepy and

wearing the knee-length *Simpsons* T-shirt I once gave her as a present. *The Simpsons* are waving at me from her chest. If I wave back, I'll topple forward on to the tiled floor.

'I've been sick,' I say.

'Have you eaten something dodgy?'

'Don't know.'

My mother puts her hand on my forehead. She wipes away the cold sweat and then rubs my back.

'Better?'

'Much better,' I say.

'Shall I make you some camomile tea?'

'No, I'm all right.'

'Are you sure?'

I try and make the word sound as convincing as possible.

'Sure,' I say, forcing a smile.

We look at each other. My mother draws herself together.

'If you feel sick again, wake me up, do you hear?'

'OK.'

She leaves the bathroom and I hear her explaining what the matter is to Robert in the hallway. As if she knew.

After a few minutes the flat is quiet again.

*Only a dream*, I think, laughing for a second at the memory of the two men who moved through it as though it were their home.

*Thanks for the visit, Elia and Aren!*

I move over to the washbasin. My knees are still shaking, but the nausea has gone. After I've splashed my face with cold water, I wash my mouth until my lips hurt. The familiar smell of the towel has more of a calming effect than my mother's hand. I dry my face, hang the towel back on the hook and look at myself in the mirror. Pale, scared and confused. Me. Too many freckles around my nose, shadows under my eyes. I can see a little bit of my mother in me, a little bit more of my father. My father. I'm told I've got his mouth. But his mouth looks completely different in the photos.

I move closer and watch myself watching myself. The eyes are tired and there are things hiding behind them. And I see myself. See myself like in one of those films you watch after a holiday where you can't really remember having done all those things you did.

I look at myself standing in the bathroom in front of this mirror. I'm still wearing my coat, so I must have just come in. My hair's messy. There's a hunted look in my eyes. I blink, lick my lips and look at my right hand holding the torn-off plant. *There you are!* I think, feeling my right arm fighting with my will. My will collapses and the hand holding the plant creeps up towards my mouth. *No!* I want to shout, but all this has already happened. This is the past, and you can't just interrupt the past or turn it back like a clock. My mouth opens, my mouth closes. I see myself swallow and now I know where the plant is hiding.

'Elia? Aren?' I whisper and go back into my room. 'Where are you?'

The room's empty.

I could look under the bed or in the cupboard, but I don't think they're hiding. I go over to the window. The cold hits me like a slap in the face. It's as though I've stuck my face into a hole in the ice. The street, two floors below me, is completely deserted.

I close the window, rub my arms and look around. There are wet patches on the floorboards – boot prints. My coat is lying on the floor, my jeans are hanging over the chair. It's a still life begging not to be disturbed, but I do disturb it and pull on my clothes with feverish fingers. I forget my gloves and my hat and fall over my trailing shoelace on the way outside. When I get out on to the street I feel dizzy for a few seconds. I can taste vomit on the roof of my mouth, my stomach rumbles loudly and then calms down. The dizziness disappears and I start to look for footprints.

*Where are they? Where's the proof that . . .*

But there aren't any footprints. The pavement in front of the block of flats hasn't been touched. Even though there's no snow falling, even though the wind isn't blowing. All the footprints have gone.

*But . . .*

I go forward a few metres and look back. My four footprints show up darkly in the snow. Are Elia and Aren still in the building? In the flat?

*Nonsense!*

*But . . .*

A snowplough approaches from the other end of the street. The motor hums, the snow makes a grinding noise as it's compacted. I look left and turn around, step in my own footprints, and look right. The street lights bathe the pavement in a yellow light. I run to the corner. There are no footprints. It's as if Elia and Aren have never been here. As though I've dreamt it.

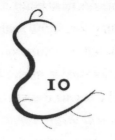

# Elia The Healer

*We can't do this to her.*

*Stay calm.*

*We shouldn't do this to her. We should tell her what—*

*That's enough, Elia.*

Aren casts me a brief glance before turning back towards Alissa. She has bunched her hands into fists and is looking around. Even from this height I can tell that she's angry. Then I hear her voice, loud and clear. Full of anger.

'Where are you?'

Her eyes search the street for our footprints. She doesn't know where to begin. She runs along the snow-covered pavement to the corner of the street, puzzled. If she only looked up . . .

'I know where the plant is!' she calls.

*So do we*, I want to reply. Aren immediately gives me a harsh look. I lower my head. We were almost certain when we entered her room. But *almost* wasn't enough. We needed proof. The smell of the plant on her skin was proof enough.

For one long minute Alissa stands angry and alone on the pavement before pulling herself together and following her own footprints back home. I can imagine her going back into her room and asking herself if it all really happened. I feel sorry for her. If only there was a way, then—

*It's time for us to go home.*

Aren swings himself down from the window sill. I follow a few seconds later. I still can't take my eyes off the girl who is disappearing into the house. The moment is brief. Long before the door has closed in the lock, I, too, have ascended into the icy winter air and spread my wings. We come to a stop on the top of the *Teufelsberg*. We have to talk before we go back. I have to sort this out before the others hear about it.

After we have landed, we straighten ourselves up and look out over the city as it awakens beneath us, pale and snowy and cold. Aren needs time to think, I hold back and wait. We've made a mistake and I don't know if we can ever make it right again.

*Do we have to make it right?*

Aren lifts his chin and breathes deeply. The wind spreads his coat out behind him. The T-shirt beneath sticks to his skin. I challenge him.

*Of course we have to make it right. We can't just leave her alone like this.*

*Maybe nothing will happen.*

*Aren . . .*

*You don't know. Maybe nothing will happen.*

*Aren, she could see us after just a couple of hours. It's already happened. Don't be naïve.*

He smiles.

*Sometimes I wish I were.*

*You know exactly what I mean.*

*Yes, I know.*

He looks at me.

*We should wait, Elia. The gift needs time. Just because this girl could see us doesn't mean a thing. Her body could still reject the gift. It takes days for it to put down roots. And until then . . .*

Aren closes his eyes and holds his face up to the wind.

*. . . we'll wait and see what happens.*

I move away from him. I don't want to see the city any more and I don't want to stand next to Aren. The mistake weighs heavy on me. It should never have got this far. From the other side of the hill I look out over the white fields.

The winter and the snow are responsible for all this.

The boy spent the holiday with his parents in Switzerland and drowned there in a river. They found his body a day later on the bank and brought it to Berlin. It was temporarily placed in the family vault because nobody wants to bury their child on Christmas Day. That could have served us well, but we couldn't get to him – the vault was closed. So we decided to visit the boy alone before the funeral. One minute would have been enough to take the gift. But just as quickly as the boy drowned in the river, Alissa broke into the vault and we came too late.

I turn away from the snowy fields and go back to Aren's side.

*Don't be angry, Elia.*

*I'm not angry, I'm frustrated. The gift grew far too quickly. How could it grow so quickly? How could it make it through the lid of the coffin? That's never happened before.*

*That's why we need to be patient.*

*But if the gift is so powerful, what will it—*

*We have to wait and see, Elia. It could still wither, it wouldn't be the first time. And if it doesn't wither – then we'll collect it as soon as everything is over.*

I shake my head.

*That's not fair on Alissa.*

*That's not the point, Elia. This has nothing to do with fairness. It's the only way.*

*We should at least tell her.*

*How do you intend to do that? How do you tell a sixteen-year-old girl that she's about to die?*

*There must be a way—*

*No, Elia, no.*

Aren puts his arm around me and we stand like that for a while on the top of the *Teufelsberg*, as a pale sun rises over Berlin to begin a new day.


A few minutes later we enter the villa from the side facing the lake.

Laika, Sohe and Avid are sitting on the terrace wrapped in blankets. They offer us a thermos flask of coffee. Aren sits down with them to explain what happened last night. I excuse myself and go inside. Herakon is reading by the fireplace and doesn't look up as I walk past.

I take the side stairs up to the second floor, because I don't want to meet anybody. I get undressed in my room and stand under the shower. I put my face into the hot stream of water and try to think about anything other than Alissa. I can't. Alissa forces her way into the foreground. She could see us. After only a few hours she could already see us. What other abilities does she have? And what will happen to her when the gift puts down roots?

I lower my head, the water beats down on my neck, the rhythm forces my thoughts onwards. We should have told her. She has a right to know. But what would that give her? Fear – nothing but fear. Maybe Aren's right and if we're lucky the gift will wither and that'll be the end of it.

'If we're lucky,' I repeat aloud, and the words sound hollow and empty under the beat of the water. They remind me of a balloon released by a child who hopes it won't fly away.

The morning is bright and clear as glass when I sit down with the others on the terrace. I can feel the wet roots of my hair immediately freeze in the cold. They crackle as I rub my hand over them.

Laika hands me a mug of coffee and says, 'You'll catch

your death.'

'Very funny,' I say, leaning back against a pillar and looking out over the lake.

Peace at last.

I'm glad when we can rest. When I spend a lot of time away from the villa it tugs at me. It's as though I've been under water for too long. I long for the moment when I can come up for air. A moment like this.

For the next few hours I don't move from the spot. I take in the view over the frozen waters of the *Wannsee*, the coming and going of the others, the conversations, the companionship – a morning at home.

The call arrives in the afternoon and I follow it.

After saying goodbye, I go down to the riverbank where Aren is already waiting for me. We're synchronized – two watches powered by the same source. I'm glad I don't have to do all this alone.

'Where?' I ask.

'*Wilmersdorf*,' says Aren, squatting down on the wall by the riverbank.

I look back and count nine ravens on the ridge of the villa's roof. There'll be other mornings like this one. I swing myself up to join him on the wall and the next moment I am pure, fluid movement.

# Part III

# Alissa The Winter Child

I put my hands around the cup and inhale the spicy scent of the coffee. The flat is quiet and my head's spinning. I can't get away from the dead boy. I can't leave the vault. Whenever I close my eyes, I see myself standing next to the coffin. Whenever I look around in my room, I expect to see two figures emerging from the shadows.

That's why I got up just before seven, feeling as though I hadn't slept at all. It was too early to call Evelin, so I showered and washed my hair. Then I sat in the kitchen and waited for the coffee to run through the machine. After the first mouthful I felt hungry and buttered two pieces of bread. The plate's empty now and the cup freshly filled. I've put my feet up on the bench and am looking out of the window. No more snow, only a blank, grey sky and cold that seems to reach out to me through the pane of glass. I don't want to go out there. Not today, not tomorrow. There are another ten days until the end of the Christmas holidays and I decide to spend every day in bed reading. Maybe I'll pretend I'm ill or even just admit I'm too lazy to move.

'Good morning.'

Robert is standing in the doorway in T-shirt and shorts, sleep in his eyes. 'Would you like some coffee?' I ask, lifting my cup.

'In a second. I just have to go to the loo.'

A few minutes later we're sitting opposite each other. We're alike, even though he's not my father and never will be. We're alike in our mannerisms. That's probably what happens when you live with somebody for a while. The way he sniffs at the coffee. Or the way he leans forward and hunches up his shoulders because he's cold.

'Is the heating on?'

'It's turned up high.'

Robert nods and takes an apple from the fruit bowl. He turns it around in his hands as though he doesn't know where to bite first.

'Get on with it,' I say.

After he's bitten into it, he grins at me.

'Are you feeling better?' he says. 'You didn't sound too good last night. I felt bad just listening. Some people aren't bothered by it. The last time I threw up, I lay on the floor for at least an hour without moving and swore never to touch alcohol again.'

'It wasn't alcohol,' I say. 'Anyway, you drink wine.'

'I swore I'd never *touch* alcohol again. I didn't say anything about drinking.'

I have to laugh, because Robert looks so funny philoso-phizing, eating an apple, hardly able to open his eyes.

'I probably ate something dodgy,' I say, pouring him some more coffee.

'Do you feel better now?'

'Much better,' I answer, rubbing my stomach absent-mindedly.

Robert inclines his head.

'You look as though you haven't slept at all.'

'I had bad dreams.'

'Do you want to talk about it?'

'I've already forgotten them.'

'Oh.'

He sips at his coffee and looks out at the backyard. I turn my cup around in my hand, glad he's stopped asking ques-tions. The boiler turns itself on in the bathroom. There are days when I could sit around forever. The heating gurgles, there's the sound of bare feet on floorboards and voices from the corridor outside the flat.

'Do you want to hear my worst dream ever?' asks Robert, looking at me again.

'Go on.'

'I can't remember any more what it was about exactly. I can only remember that I couldn't wake up. Or rather, I woke up and thought I was awake, but I wasn't.'

'How could you tell?'

'The door and the window were in the wrong place.

The whole room was strange. And I went from one dream to another. Nothing was ever right. I was scared stiff. I saw myself changing dreams as though they were TV programmes and I thought I'd never wake up properly again.'

'That's terrible,' I say. I really mean it. Just thinking about not being able to escape from a dream makes me shiver. And it gets really bad when you don't know if you've been dreaming or if something actually happened. Like yesterday. I stare into my cup. Elia and Aren. What wouldn't I give to have only dreamed about them.

'People don't have as many bad dreams if they sleep in the daytime,' says Robert.

I look at him suspiciously.

'Don't look at me like that – it's been proved.'

'Who by?'

'Some psychologist. Perhaps you should try it.'

'As long as I don't fall off my chair from exhaustion beforehand, I promise to crawl straight out of the kitchen and into bed.'

'Good girl. And if you do happen to fall off your chair, I'll carry you over there.'

'You'd really do that?'

'I'm a gentleman through and through.'

I laugh. My mum knocks on the doorframe and says, 'Am I missing something?'

'Bad coffee,' says Robert, ducking to avoid my hand.

\*   \*   \*

We chat while the two of them are having breakfast. Shortly before nine Jan comes out of his room. He sits on my lap and falls straight back to sleep. I stroke his head – his warmth makes me tired. I want to sleep for a few hours before I call Evelin. Robert lifts Jan up carefully from my lap. Jan opens his eyes straight away, of course, and seems surprised to find out that he's flying through the air.

'Where are you going?' he asks me as he lands on my mother's lap.

'I'm going back to bed for a bit.'

'Now?'

'Now.'

Jan looks from my mother to Robert and then back at me.

'But I've just woken up,' he says, confused, pointing to his left eye. When he doesn't want to run any more, he points at his feet, when he's angry, at his stomach, and when it's something to do with sleep, he points at his left eye.

I kiss his forehead and go out of the kitchen. I know exactly what will happen in my room. I'll take four steps, fall on to my mattress, pull the duvet over my head and fall asleep within ten seconds.

Good plan.

I get to my door and the phone rings. I hope it's not for me. If it's Evelin, I'll have to see her straight away. I can't go to bed first and sleep.

Jan comes running out of the kitchen. He loves answering

the phone.

'Hello! Speaking!' he says, looking at the ceiling. Then he looks at me and hangs up.

'Who was it?' I ask.

'It wasn't Simon,' says Jan, and the phone rings again.

This time Jan lifts up the receiver so carefully, it looks as though he's opening the entrance to a snake pit.

'You've got the wrong number again,' he says into the receiver, and hangs up.

'Jan!' I call.

'That wasn't Simon either,' he says, and the phone rings for the third time.

'Don't,' I tell him, and in one bound I'm standing next to him.

'If he makes you sad,' says Jan, pressing the receiver down with both hands, so that I can't answer, 'then . . .' He doesn't know what then. He only knows that Simon hasn't been in touch for the last few days. He knows I've been crying and has heard how Mum talks to me. He's doing a bad impression of her. I think he wants to protect me.

'Then what?' I ask, stroking his hair.

'Then, then . . .' stammers Jan, and then the phone rings for the fourth time.

'Then I'll build a tower that will fall down on his head.'

'Agreed.'

'Agreed?' says Jan, surprised.

'Agreed,' I say, and he gives me the receiver with big eyes.

'Yes?' I answer.

'Alissa?'

It *is* Simon. I try to smile. I shouldn't let Jan see that even the sound of Simon's voice makes me sad.

'Go and have breakfast,' I whisper to him. 'Go on.'

'Three times as high as the television tower,' murmurs Jan, moving away.

'Alissa?'

'Hi.'

'I . . .'

'Yes?'

'I need to see you.'

My smile is real now. If I had a Geiger counter in my hand, it would go wild from all the rays streaming out of me.

'What . . . I mean, when?'

'Right now,' says Simon, and suddenly starts sobbing.

I'm still holding the receiver in my hand, even though Simon hung up a long time ago. My mum's voice rings out of the kitchen. I lean my head against the wall and the past few days and weeks zoom by at incredible speed.

Simon's face. His hands. His laugh. How he waits for me outside school. Calls my name. Whispers in my ear. Asks what I'm thinking. Evelin's joy, my excitement. Dreams. I feel as though it all happened in such a short period of time. But when I think about it, it was half a year. A long six months of romance and promise and then crisis. Crisis. I can taste it in my mouth. Like running a thousand metres and wanting to be sick. Like a numb tooth and half your face feeling like rubber.

*He wants to talk to me.*

*Right now.*

*He wants me.*

I bite my lower lip. How do I look? I put down the receiver and run into the bathroom. I look terrible. Where did the shadows under my eyes come from?

*If he sees me like this . . .*

I take my make-up bag out of the cupboard. First the eyes. I start to hum and find a tune. Somebody knocks on the bathroom door.

'Alissa?'

'Mmm?'

'Evelin's on the phone.'

I must have missed the ringing. I must have been on another planet. Robert passes the phone into the bathroom. My mum hates it when I take the phone in here. I whisper a thank you to Robert and close the door again.

'Hello, you grave robber,' is how Evelin greets me.

'Hello, you.'

'What's going on?'

'Nothing.'

I look at myself in the mirror, one eye tired and normal, the other one made up as though I'm just about to walk the streets.

'Nothing at all.'

'What about our breakfast?'

'I can't.'

'But I thought—'

'I mean . . .' I interrupt Evelin and search for the right words.

'What?'

'I mean, I . . . I'm going back to bed for a bit.'

'Now?'

'I hardly slept last night.'

'Nightmares?'

'Yes.'

We both stop talking.

'Is everything all right otherwise?' asks Evelin.

I can see my mouth open and close without saying a word. There's that fish again, but this time it's gasping for words rather than water. I can't think of anything to say. I'm a really bad liar and I'm just as bad at hiding the truth.

'No breakfast?' asks Evelin again.

'I . . . I can't.'

'Oh.'

Evelin is starting to think. Her senses are alert. I know my best friend so well that I can even interpret her silence.

'Did he call?' she asks finally.

Silence.

*He.*

'Who?' I ask.

'So he called,' she says, and I answer quietly, 'Yes.'

'Oh shit!'

'It's not . . .'

'. . . what I think it is. Is that what you wanted to say?'

I want to hang up. This isn't good. This isn't good at all,
Evelin's angry.

'I'll need to see you afterwards,' I say.

'So you're meeting him?'

'We've arranged to meet.'

'Please, Alissa, he's messing with you.'

'He wants to talk to me.'

'But you know he's messing with you.'

'I . . .'

'Say it.'

'I know he messed me around, but . . .'

Silence. The *but* is hanging in the air in neon letters. I
could stretch out my hand and push my index finger through
the hole in the letter *b*.

'I don't believe it,' says Evelin, hanging up.

*But* means that I'm hopeful. It means I can't believe he
messed me around even though I know that's exactly what
he did. *But* means there's a back door, a supernatural
explanation for what I don't want to accept. Of course I
know Evelin's right. I'm not completely stupid. I also know
that part of me wants to prove her wrong. It's pure stub-
bornness. I'm stupid and idiotic and can't do anything

about it. I just can't. I'm trapped. Hope is tugging at me. I'm totally trapped.

I'm relieved that I can still look myself in the face. I take off the make-up with lotion and a cotton wool ball. Then I wash my face with soap and look at myself again. Sober and over-tired. Simon won't be getting anything more to look at than that.

'I though you were going to bed.'

My mum looks at me in surprise as I stand in the door of the kitchen, putting on my coat and woolly hat. Jan's mouth is covered in porridge. He lifts up his spoon and waves at me. Robert looks up from his magazine.

'I have to go out for a bit,' I say.

'We're leaving at twelve—'

I don't hear any more because I've turned around and crossed the hallway as though it's on fire. But I'm the one who's on fire. Inside. I'm pathetic and dramatic and on my way to the bloke who dropped out of my life two weeks ago. No calls, no letters, nothing.

Simon wanted to pick me up at home, but I said no. I need to take the underground, even if it's only one stop. I need the time to think about all this nonsense.

I get out at the *Kaiserdamm* stop and feel like one of those secret agents who turn up at the meeting point hours before to check out the lay of the land. I cross over the bridge and turn right into *Riehlstraße*. Each step produces a hard, crunching sound on the pavement. The sound changes when I enter the park. It gets softer – the snow here is almost powdered. I run over the white grass to the playground. Through the trees I can see ice skaters and a few ice hockey players chasing each other over the frozen pond. It's only now that I can hear their calls and shouts. Far away a dog barks and is silent again.

At the playground I sit down on one of the swings. I bury my hands in my coat pocket and lift my feet off the ground. Nobody is playing here, nobody is sitting on the park benches. For the next half an hour I'm alone. A man jogs by twice. He's wearing a yellow tracksuit and looks like a canary. I'd like to know why he doesn't slip on the snow. They probably make special running shoes for weather like this. After half an hour the chaotic thoughts in my head are still the same chaotic thoughts I had when I left home. I'm not in control of anything any more. I feel I'm being dragged down into a whirlpool and I want to run away. Evelin would be able to help me – she's much brighter than I am. It'd be nice to have her here now.

I push myself off the ground. The world around me rocks gently. The chain on the swing makes a grating noise. I put my head back and look up at the grey skies above me. A veil of clouds, a raven soaring on outstretched wings, calm. I feel tiredness overtaking me. What I wouldn't give to fall asleep right here. Before I lose my balance and fall off the swing, I get up and look out over the playground. I was sure that Simon would be standing there on the path. Like in a dramatic scene from a film. Entrance at the right moment with the right words and the right music for the credits.

But nobody's standing there and I still have to find the right words myself.

# Elia The Healer

She's below me. She's like a child on a swing waiting to be pushed. For a moment I'm frightened as she looks straight up at me. I know it doesn't make sense, but I think I can feel her eyes on me.

*What is she thinking? What is she feeling? When will it be time?*

I know I should keep out of this. Aren will ask questions. Aren will want to know what I'm doing here. I wanted to talk to her, but then I decided against it. The longer I watch her, the more certain I am that she should remain in ignorance. No girl wants to hear about her own death. Aren's right. I promise I will be at her side when she dies. I will ease her suffering, I will tell her I'm sorry. Until then . . .

The wind carries me away, wings spread wide, eyes focused on the city beneath me. My mind is free. Time turns into an endless moment, I am safe, I am content – until the call reaches me. I separate myself from the moment, descend and land on a window sill.

Aren lets me in.

A boy is lying in bed. He is delirious with fever. The bed-covers have slipped down to his hips, his hair is stuck to his forehead with sweat. Above his head a wooden dragon on strings moves in the draught. Aren closes the window behind me. The boy opens his eyes. He knows there's something there, he knows that he is no longer alone, but he cannot see anything.

I put my hand on his forehead and his face relaxes. Aren bends over him on the other side of the bed and pulls the blanket up over the boy's chest. Then he whispers in his ear.

'You called for us. Here we are. You're not alone. Rest.'

The boy's eyes flicker. I keep my hand on his forehead and wait for it to draw out the heat. I give the illness another two days at most – by then it will have burnt itself out. I'm sure the boy will get better. Aren picks a soft toy up from the floor where it has fallen and puts it next to the boy's pillow. We wait for a few minutes until he falls asleep.

*I saw Alissa again.*

Aren looks at me.

*And?*

I shrug my shoulders.

*She's OK, at least it looks as though she's OK. I wanted you to know that I accept your decision, Aren. It—*

I'm interrupted by another call. It's coming from the east of the city. A hospital.

Aren rubs his eyes. He hates hospitals.

*You don't have to—*

He knows he does.

We set off.

The girl is dying. It's the first time she has asked for us. For many it's like reaching for the emergency brake – they have to be really afraid before they call. Others are so anxious that they always call for help. And then there are those who never even imagine they could be helped. We only reach those when they're dead.

The girl's pupils are moving restlessly behind their lids. Her hands are clenched into fists. She doesn't want to give up. To the right of her bed a monitor is flashing, her breathing sounds strained. I pull up a chair and touch her. It's too late. I can't help her. Nobody can help her any more.

Aren takes up his place by the window. I feel his unease. The sick light that shines out of the girl makes him uncomfortable. The quiet of the room, the smell – all of this bothers him more than it does me. The helplessness, being at somebody's mercy, death patiently in pursuit of everybody.

I lower my head.

We wait.

The girl dies two hours later. I am at her side the whole time, watching over her. I don't let her out of my sight for a moment.

Afterwards I release her hands from their fists and smooth

her rumpled brow. Peaceful – only now does she look peaceful.

We take the gift with us and leave the hospital. In the woods we push some snow aside in a bright spot and lay the gift to rest.

*A fir tree?* asks Aren.

*Maybe*, I answer.

# Alissa The Winter Child

I stare alternately at the path and the trees, as though Simon might appear from behind them at any moment. I'm not expecting him to come from the direction of the pond.

'Hi.'

I turn around. A low wooden fence separates him from the playground. Ice skates hang over his shoulder. He's skated over the ice to get here more quickly.

*To be with me more quickly*, I think.

*What a load of nonsense!*

'Hi,' I say, looking at him. He seems to be waiting for me to give him permission to enter the playground. I just look at him.

'OK,' he says, swinging himself over the fence.

What happens then is a bad idea. I get off the swing. He tries to move his ice skates out of the way. I put my arms around him and smell cigarette smoke. He holds me to him. His ice skates get in the way and the sharp blades press into my chest. We laugh and move away from one another again.

My heart's racing. I can feel the nervousness in my fingertips, as if my arms have fallen asleep.

'Shall we go for a walk?'

I nod. I walk next to him and inevitably touch his hand. I feel our fingers interlace.

'Thanks for coming.'

That really makes me want to laugh. I've been a nervous wreck for two weeks because he hasn't been in touch and now he's saying thank you because I came to meet him. Is that how the world works?

Before we've walked a hundred metres, Simon stops and says, 'I'm really sorry.'

His voice sounds choked, then I see the tears.

'Simon, I—'

He shakes his head and turns away. His back twitches, he punches one hand into the other and mutters, 'What a mess, what a stupid mess!'

I put my arm around his waist and lean my head against his back. It must have been a misunderstanding. Everything will sort itself out in the next few minutes and we'll both laugh about it. Have a real laugh.

'It . . . it . . .'

Simon starts to talk without looking at me. I'd like to know what we look like to somebody watching. The way we're standing here as though we've lost each other and can't find the way back. One behind the other.

'Do you remember the party?' he asks.

Of course I remember.

We arrived at about ten. It was crowded and noisy and Evelin had already gone. I wanted to leave too, but Simon knew a lot of people there, so I stayed and danced with him and met a few of his friends. *The Fifth Element* was showing on a giant TV in one of the rooms. Soon I'd had enough of dancing and sat down with a group of people on the floor. Simon was OK with that. He kissed me and brought me something to drink and carried on dancing. That was when I lost him. He disappeared and today is the first time I've seen him since then.

'There was this girl,' he explains, shrugging his shoulders as though it was nothing.

He knew her from before – she's in this group he used to hang out with a long time ago. And when he saw this girl at the party something went wrong in his head.

'Something went wrong in my head. Believe me, Alissa, I'm not saying it's your fault or anything, but we both . . . because you wouldn't . . .'

This girl let him get closer to her than I had. She flirted with him, touched him while they were dancing, rubbed herself against him and asked if he wanted to go upstairs with her. The party was in somebody's house and the parents had gone away. So they went upstairs. And upstairs he was allowed to undress her. And he could touch her wherever he wanted. And she touched him too.

I stop leaning my forehead against his back. Simon is holding my hand tightly. I can't pull it away from his waist.

'It was so great,' he says. 'It was so . . . liberating, you know? She . . . she let me do things you don't want to do. And I did them and it was so . . .'

'Liberating,' I say, pulling my hand back.

'Yeah.'

He turns around, his eyes big and vulnerable.

'Yeah,' he repeats, and I want to hit him for that *Yeah*. I want to let all my disgust and disappointment explode by hitting his stupid face.

'I . . .'

I don't know what I want to say. It's the same feeling I had earlier when I talked to Evelin on the phone. An empty head and a longing to escape.

'But afterwards,' says Simon, catching hold of my hands, 'it was as though it hadn't happened. I knew what I'd done but I didn't know why. It . . . it was a great experience, I don't want to lie to you about that. It was really great, but I realized that it'll be better with you. I realized that we're the ones who should have done it, us two. I realized that I feel more for you than for a girl who just throws herself at me.'

He laughs, awkwardly, as though he's just told me something really personal.

'And I know I'm a bastard, Alissa. I'm a real bastard for doing it. I know that. And I'm not going to blame the alcohol even though I was very drunk. I'm not going to do that because I'm here to say sorry for being such an idiot. All I've done for the last two weeks is kick myself. I . . . I was too embarrassed to call you. I . . . I didn't want . . . No, I *couldn't* face you because I didn't want you to have anything to do with somebody like me. But then I realized I couldn't get you out of my head. Do you understand what I'm saying? That's why I'm here.'

He looks at me.

'I want you, Alissa.'

I'm dizzy. I know he's lying. I know he's— And suddenly I laugh out loud.

'You mean . . .'

I take my hands out of his and put them in front of my mouth. Oh God, I'm really hysterical.

'. . . I'm supposed to believe all that?'

'What?'

Simon's confused. This isn't going the way he planned. My laughter, my hysteria, the crazy look in my eyes. It's not that I don't believe him, but if I pretend I don't, I can shut out the truth. I'm good at that. It's not the first time I've tried to lie myself out of a difficult situation.

'It's true,' says Simon. 'Honestly, it's true. Why would I lie to you?'

My face shakes. I turn away. *Why would he lie to me? Why?* I stagger a few metres, lean against a tree and vomit.

I can feel the disgust at the back of my throat. I vomit and try to spit it out, but the only thing that comes up is my break-fast. It's disgust at the lie that masquerades as love. I never thought this could happen. I never thought I'd feel this way. It's disgust at the thought of the boy I'm in love with getting it from another girl while I'm watching *The Fifth Element*, sipping my drink.

That's what it is.

We didn't do much – we touched each other a bit and I thought that was enough. I thought Simon would think it was enough too. I'm a romantic. I don't want to give myself away just like that when I don't know if it's the right person. I've seen silly women in films who cling on to romance and they end up paying for it. Well, now I've paid for it and I hate myself for holding back. If I'd let him sleep with me, if I'd done what that other girl did, would everything be different now?

I push a handful of snow into my mouth. Simon touches my shoulder. I look at him and spit out the snow.

'It didn't mean anything,' says Simon.

# Simon The Loving One

'How can you say that?' she asks.

'Because it's true. It didn't mean anything.'

'But how can you say that?' she asks again.

'Because I love you.'

Sometimes I think she's a bit slow on the uptake. Haven't I given her a good enough explanation? Here I am, apologizing, admitting I'm a bastard, and she keeps coming out with the same old crap.

'I'm not listening to this any more,' she says, pushing me aside.

'Alissa. Wait.'

To my surprise, she waits. What now?

I run after her and stand in front of her and talk without touching her. I wish I could kiss her. Everything would be OK then. She can't resist me touching and kissing her. She knows that. That's why she's keeping her distance.

'Can't we start all over again?' I ask, avoiding her gaze. Why is she staring like that?

'Simon . . .'

'I mean, how can you just dump me like this?'

Good question. Nice move. Turn everything around and make her look like the guilty one. That takes style. You need brains to think of that.

'I'm not dumping you,' she says.

'Then give me a second chance.'

Alissa starts crying in her own unique way. She stands there without moving and cries. Doesn't cover her face up with her hands, doesn't sob loudly. Her face doesn't move. The tears run out of her eyes. Her mouth looks soft and vulnerable. I wish I could kiss her right now, lick away her salty tears. Then everything would be cool.

'Please. Don't cry,' I say, even though I like it when she cries. I liked it when she told me about her dad being dead. And I liked it when her granny went into hospital and Alissa was worried about her. It's a relief to see her crying because the rest of the time she's so unbelievably strong.

'Simon, just leave me alone,' she says, pushing past me again. 'Go back to that girl. Find yourself another girlfriend. Please.'

'There's nobody else,' I say with just the right amount of desperation. I catch up with her again. 'There's nobody else, Alissa, and I don't want there to be anybody else.'

I try to smile innocently. Last night with Silvia was great. Alissa thinks I'm an amateur but I've done it with two girls already. That's the way it should be. And Silvia's perfect for a quick shag now and then. Not as sweet as Alissa, not as good a body, but she's up for it. And she has no idea Alissa exists.

'Please,' I say.

'Piss off, will you?' she hisses at me, so I have to grab her and hold her tight.

'Why are you doing this?' I ask, feeling the anger rising.

'Because you . . .'

'Because I what?'

'Because some girl can just turn up and have sex with you while I'm watching a film. While I'm in the same house. After I kissed you. After I danced with you. After you told me how much you were in love with me. After I'd known you for half a year and thought you were the one, you were my boyfriend.'

'I *am* your boyfriend.'

'You *were* my boyfriend, Simon.'

And then she tears herself loose and leaves me there.


OK, keep calm. No problem. Let her cool off. It'll be all right. Jeez, she's difficult!

I follow her with my eyes. If she turns around she mustn't get the impression I'm taking this lightly. Only when she's disappeared behind the trees do I spit on the ground and walk towards the lake.

I run over the ice without bothering to put my skates on. I'm so pissed off. I thought it'd be a piece of cake. What's wrong with her? We didn't sign a contract, did we?

I leave the park on the other side of the lake and go into the Statt Café. The boys have gone. Their table is covered in cups and two full ashtrays. I'm glad they didn't wait. Losing a bet is one thing, paying for it straight away is something else. I go to the toilets and buy a packet of cigarettes. When I come out, the waitress is clearing our table. I could sit down and chat her up a bit. Or maybe not.

I don't want to go home, so I wander through the area, buy a hot dog from a stand on the street and eat it as I walk. I stop in front of Silvia's block of flats and go in. She opens the door to the flat after the second ring. In one hand she's holding one of those hand weights for girls. She's wearing a red top and she's sweaty.

'I'm working out,' she says, letting me in.

I light a fag and fall on to her bed. She cuddles up to me and puts her head on my lap.

'I'm glad you're back,' she says and she starts pulling at my trousers.

That's the way it should be.

## Evelin The Best Friend

Jan pushes the next book towards me.

'This is the last one,' I say.

In between tea and cake, I've been reading to him from his pile of favourite books. By now I know the stories of the little bear and his family off by heart, but I still think the pictures are funny.

'This is the last one,' says Jan, holding up one finger. 'And then another one, OK?'

He doesn't wait for my answer and looks through the box of books he's dragged into the kitchen. I look at the clock. It's twelve and there's still no sign of Alissa.

'You're welcome to wait longer,' says her mother, lifting Jan up from the floor.

'No!' says Jan.

'Oh yes,' says his mother.

'Help!' cries Jan, stretching his arms out towards me.

Robert comes into the kitchen wearing his coat and Jan moves over to his arms.

'In case you do see Alissa,' says Robert to me, 'tell her we won't be coming back till late. We never manage to escape from my sister in under four hours.'

Robert's sister lives seventy miles north of Berlin. To Alissa she's Aunt Doris. Aunt Doris is as highly strung as Robert is calm. The last time Alissa was there was at Easter. She told me that visiting her aunt left her feeling as jittery as if she'd drunk countless cups of coffee. It might also have had something to do with her aunt's three dachshunds, who bark hysterically as soon as you stop stroking them.

'I'll let her know,' I promise.

Soon afterwards I'm alone in the flat. A few minutes later I've already had enough of waiting and write Alissa a note. I put it on her pillow before heading for home. I hope she's not angry with me for hanging up on her this morning. Sometimes I can't help it, especially where that loser Simon is concerned. I hope he rots in hell.

Alissa's sitting on the top step in front of our house with a newspaper under her bum. I can see what sort of state she's in. She just sits there, staring at nothing. When she notices me, she lifts her head involuntarily. Her eyes are red, her mouth narrow and hard.

'Fancy some tea?' I ask.

She gets up without taking her hands out of her coat pockets. She must be freezing cold.

'Been waiting long?'

She shrugs her shoulders and looks at the newspaper at her feet as if one of the pages might tell her how long she's been standing here.

'Was it bad?'

She knows I'm not talking about the wait and sniffs without answering. Yeah, it must have been pretty bad.

'Come on.'

I put my arm around her and feel her shivering. Why didn't she go inside? She knows where the spare key's hidden. I look at her out of the corner of my eye and can see that this is really serious. There's only one thing that helps straight away in situations like this.

'Better?'

Alissa stretches out and takes the mug. The bath foam around her crackles.

'Much better,' she says.

I've set up a lamp and put some bergamot oil in it. Candles are burning, the new CD by the *Eels* is coming quietly out of the speakers and Alissa has told me everything. She even described Simon's lying face in detail and let out all her bitterness in those few sentences. Then she cried and sank down into the water up to her chin. The only thing that moved after that was her eyes.

Now she's sipping tea and asks me what I think about it all.

'You don't want to know,' I say.

'Yeah, I do. Just make it interesting.'

'OK,' I say, tucking a strand of hair behind my ear. First of all I'd pretend the guy's dead. Completely dead. I wouldn't talk to him, I wouldn't look at him, I'd wipe him out of my memory.'

'Good.'

'And then I would make it very clear to myself that I'm not responsible for any of it.'

That touched a nerve. I can see her wince.

'Yes. But if I'd—'

I interrupt her. 'If you'd let him do it, the same thing would have happened, sooner or later. Just because the guy's horny, that doesn't mean you have to have sex with him. What kind of love is that?'

'I know, but . . .'

She shuts up and I'm glad. Talking somebody out of a complex isn't easy, especially when the person is as stubborn as Alissa.

'I could lie here all day,' she says.

'You *can* lie there all day,' I say.

She nods. I get the feeling she's relieved. It wasn't the perfect change of topic, but it doesn't matter.

'About this morning . . .'

I turn my head in the direction of the hallway where our phone is.

'. . . I'm sorry I hung up. Sometimes I can't help it. You make me so mad.'

'I know that feeling,' she says. 'I even get pissed off with myself sometimes.'

She gives me the empty mug. I fill it up and give it back to her.

'I wish I was like you,' she says.

'Dream on!'

'No, really. I think things would be easier that way.'

'You mean it's easier to go out with girls than to go out with boys?'

'You seem pretty happy.'

'I am happy, but that doesn't mean it's easier. I've just had more luck up till now.'

'I could use some luck.'

'Hey, Alissa.'

I reach into the water and grab hold of her free hand.

'Simon was a mistake, OK? It'll get better.'

'How do you know that?'

'Intuition and magic. My witch's blood tells me.'

I feel as though a shadow has wandered over Alissa's eyes.

'Sometimes,' she says, squeezing my hand, 'I'm sure you know much more than me.'

'Hey, less of the sometimes. I do know a lot more than you. I'm older.'

'One month and eleven days.'

'One month and eleven days are a lot when you're sixteen.'

We laugh. I pull my hand out of the water and dry it on a towel. Alissa closes her eyes. There are tiny beads of sweat on her forehead, face and shoulders. A drop rolls down her throat and disappears into the foam. I'm sure that I love her.

'There's something else,' says Alissa, barely audible.

I wait. She keeps her eyes closed as she continues talking.

'When I fell through the snow yesterday, there . . . there was something there. There was the vault and there were paths leading off to rooms. There was something in one of the rooms.'

Alissa looks at me.

'Do you want to hear this?' she asks me suddenly.

'What? Why do you think I wouldn't want to hear it?' I reply.

'Maybe because I don't want to talk about it,' she answers, closing her eyes again.

A minute goes by and then another.

When Alissa starts to tell the story, I draw my knees up on to the chair without realizing and clasp my arms around them.

# Alissa The Winter Child

'Come on, then,' I say, sliding backwards in the bath so that there's room for her. The air on my breasts feels pleasantly cold, the crackling made by the foam sounds like a radio station fading out. Evelin takes her trousers off. She puts her knickers, socks and watch on top of her clothes.

'Here we go . . . Aaah, that's nice!'

'Not too hot?'

'No, just right.'

We both sink down into the water up to our chins. Our thighs touch and our knees peek out like islands. I'd much prefer not to talk about Elia or Aren or the plant for the next few minutes. But after a couple of seconds Evelin says, 'I'm scared.'

'You're not the only one,' I say.

'And the two of them disappeared just like that?'

'I don't know how they did it. I've no idea how they even got in. The door to the flat's always locked. It was locked when I ran out. But I couldn't find any trace of them. There was nothing in front of the main entrance to the building and nothing on the pavement either.'

Evelin exhales loudly. Her breath moves the foam under her chin.

'Elia and Aren,' she says, as though by saying the names out loud she could bring them to life. 'Who do you think they are?'

I've gone through all the possibilities in my head, beginning with aliens right the way through to secret agents hunting for an escaped virus. Just like *The X Files*.

'I have no idea,' I answer. 'They knew about the plant. They knew that I had it. They could smell it on me and they told me none of it was my fault. The plant wanted me to take it and . . .'

'. . . swallow it?' says Evelin.

'. . . and swallow it,' I say.

'But why?'

'I don't know.'

'And how can a plant . . .'

I don't hear any more. I've just realized why I swallowed the plant. For a second this thought wanders through my head like a coded message . . . *to hide it, so that* . . . I don't get any further. I lose the thread and I sit there and watch Evelin's mouth open and close.

'. . . do now?'

'What?'

'I asked what you want to do now.'

101

I don't have an answer to that either. Elia and Aren have disappeared, I vomited up the plant, end of story. If the two of them are still interested in the plant, they can poke round in the drains.

'I don't know,' I say.

'What if they come back?'

I shake my head.

'They heard me throwing up. I'm positive they knew what was going on right away. And besides, they wouldn't have disappeared if I'd still had the plant.'

I touch my stomach without realizing. Evelin nods. 'Right.'

She looks down at the foam and then looks back at me.

'They won't come back,' I say with certainty.

'They've gone for good,' says Evelin.

'Weird,' I say.

'Creepy,' she says. Then we just lie in the water not saying anything, not looking at each other. I've got no idea what's going on in Evelin's head, but I keep seeing Elia and Aren in my room. I can still feel the burning in my throat from throwing up.

*They've gone for good.*

*What if they haven't?*

*Then . . .*

*And why wasn't I afraid of them?*

*Their touch. They touched . . .*

*And why did they think I couldn't see them?*

Evelin runs more hot water. We look at each other and

speak almost at the same time.

'What I don't underst—'

'What I wanted to sa—'

'You first.'

'OK', says Evelin, turning off the tap. 'What I don't understand is how a plant can grow out of a dead person. If that was normal, it'd be in some biology textbook, wouldn't it?'

'It isn't in any of the biology textbooks I've ever seen,' I say.

'Nobody's ever pointed it out to me either. Are you sure that it—'

'Evelin,' I interrupt, 'the plant was growing right out of the boy's chest. It was as if it had put down roots. I could feel it when I pulled on the stem that was left behind.'

'Yuk! Stop it.'

I wipe my face and sink deeper into the bath. Suddenly I feel cold in the hot water.

'What were you going to say?' asks Evelin.

'I've been thinking and I know this sounds strange, but would you come back to the cemetery with me?'

'You think they're there?'

'Maybe there's somebody there I can talk to about it,' I answer. 'It's important to me.'

Evelin lifts one hand out of the water and pats my knee.

'That's my girl,' she says. 'A fighter. That's the way I like you.'

\* \* \*

It's the afternoon when we get to the cemetery. We go in through the main entrance like ordinary people, and follow the paths, which have been swept clear of snow, to the mausoleum. The flowers and the presents have disappeared. When I try the door, it opens easily. The entrance room is deserted. Some stairs lead down. I stay where I am. There's no way I'm going down the steps to the vault.

'Are you looking for the little boy's funeral?' asks a woman walking past with an old man leaning on her arm.

Evelin nods. I can't move.

'They brought it forward,' continues the woman. 'It's supposed to snow again later this afternoon.'

She points to one of the paths.

'If you hurry, you'll be able to give his family your condolences.'

'Thank you,' says Evelin, and pulls at my hand.

'I don't want to,' I say, not moving from the spot.

'But—'

'We have no reason to be there,' I interrupt.

The real reason is that I don't want to get close to that boy again. I don't want to see the coffin. I thought this was a good plan before, now I feel like I'm making a mistake. I want to get rid of the boy's spirit, so I can sleep in peace again. I don't want to see where's he's being buried.

'But maybe Elia and Aren are at the funeral,' says Evelin.

We look at each other. She's so damn logical. She lets go of my hand and slips her arm through mine.

'Just for a minute,' she says, pulling me away from the mausoleum.

There's a small group of people standing around the open grave. We can't see the coffin. A few of the mourners are holding hands. Others are looking at the ground with vacant expressions. Elia and Aren aren't there.

'Come on,' I say. 'That's enough. Let's go.'

We disappear the same way we came. Nobody noticed us. Only when we've left the cemetery can I breathe easily again.

'Do you believe me?' I ask, standing still.

Evelin hasn't questioned my story about the plant and Elia and Aren one bit. I realize how much I doubt what happened last night. How much do I really believe? How much do I wish that Evelin would laugh and tell me I've made it all up?

*A lot.*

'I know you,' answers Evelin. 'You could never make up something like that. Your imagination's far too limited.'

I nudge her shoulder and she puts her arm around me.

'So we can forget about it?' I ask uncertainly, without looking at her. She has to make the decision for me.

'Let's forget about it,' says Evelin, hugging me tight.

I don't feel like going home, so we take the underground to *Adenauer Platz* and hang out in Video World for a while. Then we have a falafel at the Arab place around the corner before getting back on the underground. We've chosen *Con*

*Air* and *Sommersby*. Evelin wanted an action film and I wanted something romantic. I should know better.

'You should know better,' says Evelin.

'I'm still hopeful,' I say.

'You're soppy,' she says.

Evelin's mum gets up and leaves after ten minutes of *Con Air*. Then her dad comes in and says, 'Anya said this was my kind of film.'

He sits down next to us on the sofa. We pass round crisps and salt sticks and watch the action.

In the break we make hot chocolate and get ready for the romantic part of the evening. Evelin's parents swap places. At the end of the film her mum and I sit there crying, while Evelin yawns and gets a cushion thrown at her head.

'You'll never be liberated women,' she says.

'That's what we've got you for,' retorts her mum. Then she asks me if I want to stay overnight. I look over at Evelin. Evelin nods. We understand each other.

'Another time,' I say.

I haven't had any time to think. Too much has happened all at once. Elia and Aren aren't the only ones on my mind – I also have to sort out what's happening with Simon. Evelin telling me to forget him doesn't help much. I don't think you can just forget somebody, no matter what kind of crappy things he's done. That's like closing your eyes and not wanting to see any more.

It's after ten when I say goodbye to Evelin. It reminds me

of the previous evening when I said goodbye, only this time I'm not taking a secret with me. My best friend and I are open with each other, we tell each other everything. I hope I'll have a boyfriend like that one day. I have to. I just need faith, courage and a bit of luck. I'm a romantic through and through.

# Simon The Loving One

Eric lives two flats below us. No matter what I do, he always knows when I come home. So I've come in, I've just taken off my shoes and stuck my head round the living room door, when the doorbell rings.

'I'll go,' I say to my parents and open the door.

'Well?' asks Eric.

I pull a fiver out of my jeans and hand it over.

'Mate, I knew it!'

'Enjoy the rest of your day,' I say, trying to close the door.

'Hey, Simon mate, chill!' says Eric. He tells me the boys are downstairs in his flat watching a video and would I fancy drinking a beer with them and having a little smoke of something?

'Come on,' he says.

I want to go straight to bed. I've got a really bad headache from listening to Silvia blabbing on. That's why I left so quickly. But I can't just go to bed. As soon as Eric tells the boys I've lost the bet, they'll all be standing here asking for their fivers. I might as well get it over with in one go. And I really fancy a smoke.

'OK,' I say, closing the door without waiting to see what Eric's reaction is.

I pinch a packet of sausages from the fridge and half a bottle of vodka from the freezer. There's no better way to forget a girl than getting off with somebody else or getting wasted. I'm doing both. You don't get much cooler than that.

We start talking a third of the way into the film. John Carpenter's *Vampires* is a piece of crap. If it wasn't for all the blood flying through the air, we'd have turned it off a long time ago.

I tell the boys what happened with Alissa. How she cried and then ran off.

'You have to let some girls off the leash, otherwise they'll keep trotting along after you,' says Alex, helping himself to one of the sausages.

'I'd like to get her back on the leash,' I say.

Eric pushes out his lower lip and nods. I know he fancies Alissa and would be really chuffed if he could get it together with her.

'Don't even think about it,' I warn him.

'What are you on about?'

'You know exactly what I'm on about.'

Martin opens his mouth for the first time that evening.

'She's definitely a lesbian.'

'Bullshit,' I say.

'Come on! That lezzie she hangs out with fancies her rotten. You could be blind and still notice.'

'You're talking crap,' I say. 'You're worse than the film.'

'The film's really crap,' says Alex, turning off the TV.

Suddenly it's quiet in Eric's room. I wish the telly was still on.

'Don't you think so?' says Martin.

'What?'

'You know, that she's a lesbian.'

'Come off it.' I get angry. 'I should know.'

Eric whistles. The others laugh.

'If she was my girlfriend . . .' says Martin, before falling silent.

Alex shakes his head.

'You'll never get that lucky.'

'Then what?' I want to know. Martin's beginning to get on my nerves.

'I'd show her what's what,' he says. 'It's not normal for her to hang out with that Evelin. What are you waiting for? To see them shove their tongues down each other's throats? Any idiot can see they're practically joined at the hip.'

Now I laugh too.

'How am I supposed to know that? Do you expect me to change schools so I can keep an eye on them or what?'

Martin is silent and takes a swig of beer.

'What do you think I should do?' I persist. Now let's see

him come up with something clever.

'Don't ask me,' he says. 'No skin off my arse. It's your problem, mate.'

'Exactly,' I say and knock back my vodka.

They won't stop talking about Alissa. I'm under siege. And I'm getting angrier by the minute. I've let myself be dis-respected. Alissa really is a tart. The way she left me stand-ing there as though we didn't know each other. I had plans. I wanted to move in with her. I was crazy about her. Still am. It doesn't just stop like a TV series. No, this is real life. It doesn't just stop.

'You shouldn't have stood for it,' says Alex at one point.

I nod. I shouldn't have bet that I'd get her back just like that either. I should have kept my mouth shut. I've just coughed up three fivers for it.

'If she was my girlfriend . . .' Martin says for at least the tenth time.

I look at him.

'If you say that again,' I warn him, 'I'll punch you.'

'Me?'

He taps a beer bottle against his chest.

'Don't you know who I am?' he asks me.

'A giant arse,' I say.

'Hey!'

Martin gets to his feet angrily.

'I'm your mate and you're having a go at me because of

some silly cow. You need to sort your life out!'

'Hey, calm down,' says Eric. 'Martin, sit down.'

Martin sits down again. We look at each other.

'Apologize to him,' Eric says to me.

'Sorry,' I say.

'That's OK.'

Martin leans forward so we can clink bottles.

'Are you drinking that by yourself?' asks Alex.

I look at the vodka bottle, surprised. There's only a bit left in the bottom.

'This is all for me,' I say, and the boys laugh and we clink bottles in a circle.

'At least something belongs to you,' says Martin.

I grin. I'm too drunk to hit him.

The dope's ancient. You can tell from the first drag. The joint lights up as though it's been dipped in alcohol. That's how it tastes too.

'Where did you get this stuff?' we ask Eric.

He waves the question away. He's right, it's better than nothing.

'Pride,' says Alex, 'is the only thing you shouldn't let anybody take away from you.'

'Exactly,' I say.

'I'd never talk to her again,' says Martin.

'Oh, I dunno,' says Eric.

'Don't even think about it,' I say, warningly, passing the

joint on to Alex.

'Stop it,' says Eric, without looking at me.

'They're all tarts,' says Martin.

'Exactly,' I say.

'Pride is everything' says Alex.

'Oh, I dunno,' says Eric.

The others are staying the night. Why don't you stay as well? they say. But I don't want to crash at Eric's. I want to go home. Two floors up and into bed. And then I do something strange. I go in the wrong direction. I'm like a balloon, but like the opposite of a balloon. I don't fly up but down. Down the stairs and out of the house. It's all crap.

My leather jacket isn't very warm. I bury my hands in my trouser pockets, scratch my balls and hunch up my shoulders. It's snowing again. It snows every day. Totally ice age. Where are my cigarettes? Shit, I've left my cigarettes at Eric's. I can't go back there now. Keep going then. This crappy snow just won't stop falling. This is exactly the sort of weather for sitting at home and listening to music by candlelight with Alissa lying next to me, and then we talk and I put my hand on her stomach and feel it rising and falling, and then my hand is on her breast and I can feel her heartbeat and Alissa says *That's nice, Simon*, and I ask, *What about this?* and then she says *No, Simon,* and I say *OK* because it is OK. She's so sweet, she's my angel, and she . . .

I stumble, fall into the snow up to my knees and get up again. At least in this weather you can't put your foot in any dog shit. It sinks through the snow, freezes, and only turns up again in spring. That's the way it should be.

What now?

The hot dog stand at the courthouse is still open. I want a chilli burger, but I feel as though everybody's looking at me strangely. So I don't get one. I cross over to the other side of the street and get a hot dog from the Mexican place. It's really crap the way they stick those things in the microwave. I can't stand the ping the machines make. It tastes like heated-up plastic. I wolf the thing down. Now I'm going to . . .

I don't know what I'm going to do.

And then I remember.

Remember again.

Alissa.

My hands shake as I tear the plastic off the new pack. I stick a cigarette between my lips and search through my jacket and can't find my lighter. Where am I going to get a light? I keep the cigarette in my mouth. Better than nothing. I stand in the entrance to a block of flats, away from the wind.

And wait.

And it gets colder.

And I wait.

And my hands are fists and I'm so angry I start to cry, that's how angry I am. All my pride. Gone. Martin said so. Shit!

What a fool. I keep crying. If it gets any colder I'll get pneumonia. That'd make Alissa cry. But that'll take a while.

And I wait.

And cry.

And decide to go.

And decide to stay.

And wait.

I build a missile. I build a bad-ass one. The snow's just right, this one's gonna fly. I pack the snow together tight and soon I've got the perfect snowball. It's got an ice crust from the heat of my hands. Yeah, it's a bad-ass missile. I throw the snowball into the air and catch it. Just the right weight. I press my lips against it and lick the ice. And start crying again.

At last.

I thought the night was already over. I thought I'd wake up in my bed. Then footsteps come closer, crunching their way up the street, and I creep out. I was always good at that. Like a cat. I slip a couple of times and once I'm really clever and take a short cut. Instinct. I follow my instinct. Not everyone would do that. Then I wait again. In a doorway, behind a car, always well-hidden. Seventeen years old and totally crazy. I start to giggle. The snowball vibrates in my hand, I laugh so much that I start crying again. That's enough now. The steps get closer. They're cautious on the icy pavement. A cat. The snow's falling on all sides. It's so cold and the city's so quiet.

It's as though it isn't a city at all. A city in a glass ball. Turned upside down. A shadow runs past. I wait and straighten myself up behind the car. See her, smell her. Coat and hair, a grey wisp of breath that dissolves into nothing before my eyes. And then she disappears – five metres, ten metres. And I can still smell her and I prepare myself and say it quietly:

'Alissa.'

And she turns around.

# Alissa The Winter Child

I only feel the pain when I open my eyes. It feels as though my head has split open along the parting in my hair. I blink and the stars in front of my eyes turn into explosions of light and slowly fade away.

'Alissa.'

I look to my right and see Simon. He's crouching next to me, his hands on his knees.

Am I lying down? Where am I lying?

I look up at him. Snowflakes drift past his shoulders. Behind him I can see a street light and the night sky.

He strokes my hair.

'I'm sorry,' he says.

I don't know what he's talking about. I try to get up. Simon pushes me back to the ground.

'What are you doing?' I ask.

'My pride . . .'

Simon puts his hand on his chest.

'. . . gone.'

He laughs. I can smell his breath.

'You're drunk,' I say, pushing his arm away.

'Drunk on love,' he says, bending over to kiss me. He loses his balance and falls on top of me. My arms are trapped between us. I try to push him off me. He laughs again.

'Wait,' he says. 'Let's get comfortable.'

He's got me pinned down. Only my legs and my head are free.

'Shall I light a few candles?' he asks.

His face is only a couple of centimetres away from mine. His pupils are dilated. His mouth is shaking.

'Simon,' I say, 'we're lying in the middle of the street!'

He looks around in surprise.

'Oh.'

He smiles down at me.

'What are we doing here?' he asks, and in the same moment I manage to raise my left knee and ram it between his legs.

He curls up into a ball and slides off me. When I try to get up, he grabs me by the hair.

'You little . . . *you whore!*'

He jerks my head back, I scream, he puts his other hand over my mouth, I can see tears in his eyes.

'If you scream . . .'

He doesn't finish the sentence. His face is cold and angry, but there's sadness there as well. And that's something I don't want to see because his sadness awakens my sympathy.

There's something not quite right with me.

'OK?' he asks.

I nod. He takes his hand off my mouth.

'I guess we're finished then?' says Simon, completely rational for a moment.

I pull in my bottom lip, I could cry, I nod again.

'I loved you,' says Simon.

'I loved you too,' I say quietly.

'Crappy world,' says Simon.

I can't think of anything to say to that because as far as I'm concerned he's the one who made a crappy world out of this wonderful one and not the other way around.

'I . . . I'll clear off then?'

'OK,' I say.

'Don't you want to kiss me goodbye?'

I know it would be wise to say *Yes* and say, 'No.'

'As if you had a choice,' says Simon. There's that laugh again – slightly crazy, slightly deranged.

'Please,' I say, trying to turn my face away, but he's holding me by the hair.

'For goodbye's sake,' he says and kisses me.

I feel his cold lips. I feel the warm wetness of his tongue. I could bite it, but I keep still and let it happen, completely passive.

*It'll be over in a minute, it'll be over—*

Suddenly Simon pulls his head back and jumps up. He laughs nervously, touches his mouth and throws me a last look – with his eyes wide open – before he runs off.

A few minutes later I take my coat off, pull off my boots and go into the living room. My mum's still awake. She's sitting on the sofa with a detective novel. I put my aching head in her lap and close my eyes. When I feel her fingers in my hair, all my chaotic thoughts fall away. For one never-ending minute my mind is free and clear.

'Everything OK?' asks my mum.

I nod, bury my head in her lap and lie still. I wish she'd keep reading and act as if I'm not there. I want to think about everything in peace.

'Have you had a fight with Evelin?'

I shake my head.

*Just keep reading, Mum. Please.*

Her fingers touch my cheek.

'Alissa, you're crying.'

I get up and go to my room without looking around, without saying goodnight. Enough. I fall into bed in my clothes, curl up into a ball, and pull the blankets up over my head.

*Peace.*

Peace and time to think.

*Finally.*

Five and a half hours later I wake up bathed in sweat. The peace and the sleep haven't helped. I didn't relax for one second. My jeans are sticking to my legs. At some point I must have taken off my jumper. I've sweated so much that I've started to freeze. I get up, take a pair of knickers and a T-shirt out of the wardrobe and open the window to let in some air. The night's over.

The shower does me good. At last I manage to relax and put my thoughts in order. A quarter of an hour later I carry the phone through the hallway into my bedroom and call Evelin. She picks up on the second ring and doesn't ask who it is. She only says, 'Alissa, what are you doing? What time is it?'

'You don't really want to know,' I answer, picturing her switching on the light to look at her alarm clock.

'It's . . . six twenty-one,' says Evelin. 'Thanks a lot.'

'I'm sorry.'

Evelin sighs.

'What's the matter?'

'Nothing good,' I say, and tell her about Simon's attack.

'Oh no,' says Evelin. 'What a prick!'

I laugh, but then I feel how the laugh turns around in my throat and becomes a sob.

'Hey,' says Evelin. 'Shall I come over?'

'No, no, it's OK. I . . . I just don't know what to do.'

'If you ask me, you should call the police.'

'I can't do that.'

'Listen, if that idiot can lie in wait for you at night, what's the next stunt he's going to pull?'

I'm silent and picture how my mum would react. She'd call

the police without a moment's hesitation.

'Do you want to be my bodyguard?' I ask.

'Do I look like Kevin Costner?' asks Evelin in reply.

'Kevin Costner's a softie.'

'Do I look like a softie?'

I grin. I'm so glad I phoned her. My Evelin.

'I feel much better now,' I reassure her. 'I . . . I was thinking things over in the shower and I think I'm all right again now. It's over with Simon. Definitely over, I promise you. I'm not that stupid. It's over. That's what I wanted to tell you.'

Evelin exhales loudly.

'I'm glad to hear it,' she says.

'Thanks again for everything. Go back to sleep, OK?'

I hang up after we've said goodbye and sit on the bed for a moment, satisfied. It's true, I really do feel better.


Some things are like illnesses. You have to get them out of your body, sweat them out, get over them. If there wasn't any snow I could go jogging in the park. I feel a desperate need to move. I want to get Simon the illness out of my system. So I decide to make a small contribution to family life.

Jan catches me before I can even leave my room. He's standing in the doorway holding his cuddly tortoise in one hand. His pyjama jacket has slid upwards and his trousers are hanging low so that I can see his bellybutton.

'Are you going away?' he asks.

'No, I'm going to buy some fresh rolls.'

'With me?'

'If you get dressed quickly.'

'OK!'

In the end I have to put his clothes on for him. He chatters away incessantly and tries to put a sock over the tortoise's head. When I've finished dressing him, he has to go to the toilet. I pull his trousers down and sit on the edge of the bath till he's finished.

'Flush,' I say.

'OK,' says Jan.

He flushes and his tortoise falls into the toilet at the same time.

'Oh no!' he says, pressing his hands over his ears as though he can't bear to hear the tortoise's cries for help.

We wash the tortoise off in the shower, hang it over the hot water pipes and go into the corridor, where I sit down on the floor.

'This is the left one,' I say, holding out Jan's boot. 'And this is the right one.'

'OK,' says Jan, as though that's no problem.

For weeks his favourite word has been OK. If he could he wouldn't say anything else. My mother doesn't think it's funny at all and warns him every time he says it. As soon as she's out of earshot, Jan produces one OK after the other with a big grin on his face.

When I've finished putting his clothes on and am about to tie my bootlaces, Jan runs to the front door and fiddles around with the lock.

'Wait!' I call.

'OK,' he answers, opening the door.

'Jan?'

No reply. He's standing up straight in the crack of the door, one hand on the handle as if he's holding on tight to a rope. I fasten my boots, get up, and take my coat down from the hanger. I can hear Jan whispering. Then he closes the door and leans against it.

'What's the matter?' I ask.

'All the bakeries are closed,' he answers, bending over to undo the Velcro fastenings on his boots.

'What are you doing?'

He shrugs his shoulders and says again quietly, 'All the bakeries are closed. Sorry.'

'Move over,' I say, pressing down the handle. He moves over reluctantly, so that I can open the front door.

'What . . . ?'

I don't get any further, because Simon's lying in front of the door, knees drawn up to his chest, head between his arms, asleep.

'Oh shit!' The words slip out of me.

'He's dead now,' says Jan, pulling at my jeans.

'What?'

'He's dead now, so close the door.'

'He's not dead, Jan.'

Jan squints through the crack in the door.

'What's he doing then?'

'He's asleep,' I say.

'Hasn't he got a bed?'

'Yes, but . . .'

I don't know what to tell him.

'Go inside now,' I say instead.

'What about you?' asks Jan.

'I'll think of something,' I answer.

It's probably not the best something I ever thought of, but it's definitely better than a frozen bloke who used to be my boyfriend lying on our doorstep.

First I fetch a box of Lego for Jan, then I wake Robert up and together we carry Simon into the flat, where we lie him on my bed. Robert tries to wake him, but soon gives up. We leave the door open a crack so that we can hear when he comes round.

'I thought it was over between you two,' says Robert when we're both sitting down at the table.

'It *is* over,' I say, annoyed.

Robert looks at me in surprise.

'Sorry,' I say, sliding around nervously on my chair. If I didn't think my mother would come in at any minute, I'd tell him the whole story immediately.

I get up and close the kitchen door. That's better.

'Last night . . .' I begin, and tell him what happened.

'Bastard!' says Robert afterwards.

I shrug my shoulders and look down at the patterns on the tabletop.

'As far as I'm concerned we can put him right back outside in the corridor,' Robert adds.

Then the kitchen door opens. It's Simon.

'Alissa,' he says.

And comes inside.

And kneels down in front of me.

And kisses my hand.

# Robert The Stepfather

For a few seconds nothing happens. Simon kneels in front of Alissa and kisses her hand. It's actually quite hilarious. A gallant joke by somebody in love, only this lover has spent the night in front of our front door – in the middle of winter, when the temperature outside is minus seventeen degrees.

'Simon, come on, that's enough,' I say.

Alissa tries to pull her hand back. Simon holds on to it tightly and licks her finger. I jump up. Alissa slides her chair back. Now Simon has her left index finger in his mouth. His eyes are closed. He's kneeling on the ground, looking crazy, sucking her finger.

'For God's sake, Simon! That's—'

Before I can do anything, Alissa has slapped him with her right hand. Her fingers plop out of his mouth. He opens his eyes, surprised. I walk around the table, put my arm around Alissa protectively and draw her away.

'Simon, pull yourself together!'

He's not listening to me, he does exactly the opposite – he puts his hands in front of his face and starts to cry. That's precisely the moment when Sarah comes in.

'Oh, good grief!' she says.

'Don't get worked up,' I say.

'Why shouldn't I get worked up? What's Simon doing on our kitchen floor?'

I tell her how Alissa found him in front of our door. Then Sarah goes over to Simon, puts her arm around him, and says, 'Please get up.'

Simon gets up, but doesn't take his hands away from his face.

'You have to go home now,' says Sarah, leading the sobbing Simon out of the kitchen.

She does it with great dignity. Alissa and I watch the two of them. Shortly afterwards the door to the flat bangs shut and Sarah comes back into the kitchen. She's furious.

'What's the matter?' I ask.

'What's the matter?' she asks back. 'Maybe that's what Alissa should be telling us. That boy's a wreck.'

She looks at Alissa. 'What did you do to make him crawl around here on all fours like a faithful puppy?'

I react much too slowly. Before I can even move a finger, Alissa has disappeared from the kitchen. The bedroom door slams. I meet Sarah's gaze and say, 'That was really stupid of you.'

We talk. After I've told her what happened between Alissa

and Simon, I immediately see the doubt in Sarah's eyes.

'How can you *not* believe her?' I ask.

'Why should I believe her? Simon's a nice boy. Just because he doesn't want to go out with her any more doesn't mean he's lost his marbles.'

I feel as though I've stumbled into the wrong film.

'You didn't just say that,' I say.

'Of course I just said that.'

'You think Alissa's lying?'

Sarah doesn't reply.

'Answer me,' I demand.

Sarah shrugs her shoulders and hedges by saying, 'I don't know.'

'That's not good enough.'

'What do you want me to say?'

'Tell me whether you believe her or not.'

'I . . . I don't know.'

'Alissa doesn't lie. You know that, don't you?'

'I don't know anything.'

'Christ!' I say, walking out of the room.


A few minutes later I'm sitting opposite Sarah again. I checked to see what Jan was doing and then had two quick drags of a cigarette on the balcony. This woman drives me crazy.

'Have you thought about it?' I ask.

'I'm sorry,' she says. 'It just touched me, the way Simon

was kneeling there. He looked as though he was begging. I . . .'

She breaks off.

'You should talk to her,' I say.

She nods but doesn't make any move towards getting up.

'Do it now,' I add.

Sarah looks up. I know that look. *Can't you do it for me?* her eyes ask. I could, but I'm not going to.

'Get on with it,' I say.


Their voices float quietly out of the bedroom. The door's slightly ajar. I wish Sarah had closed it behind her. I get up, creep along the corridor, and close it. I look in on Jan again before going out on to the balcony. God, am I tense! I fish the hastily extinguished cigarette out of the ashtray and light it again. There's no snow falling today, no sun either – just a grey sky and a quiet that hangs in the air like acoustic smog. A few tyre tracks point to the fact that this is a normal work-ing day. I don't want to think about work.

I can hear the kettle being filled up back in the flat. That was quick. Hopefully Sarah's managed to pull herself together and have a sensible talk with Alissa. Sometimes it scares me to see how much the two of them avoid each other. If Alissa and I had problems, OK, that would be understand-able, but it doesn't make any sense for the two of them to still be at loggerheads.

I smoke the cigarette down to the filter and press the stub

into the snow on the balcony wall. It makes a hissing sound.
I put the stub into the ashtray and am just about to turn
around when I see Simon standing in the doorway directly
opposite our building. He's standing in the shadows – a cloud
of breath gives him away. I wait, watch him hop from one
foot to another, see his arms folded in front of his chest.

*The boy's lost his marbles*, I think and decide not to
mention it to Alissa.

# Sarah The Mother

'I'm sorry.'

I sit down next to her on the floor. There's cold air coming in through the window and I ought to remind her that the heating's on full blast. But this is the wrong moment to get worked up about heating bills. Robert would bite my head off.

Alissa doesn't look at me.

'Honestly,' I say, putting my hand on her arm. 'I'm sorry.'

We sit like this for a while – Alissa with her face turned away, as though she's reading something in the grey skies, and me next to her with a bad back. Robert and I need a new mattress. Every morning my back's as stiff as a board. We urgently need a new mattress.

'Simon looked so pitiful,' I try to explain.

Alissa looks at me and says, 'Robert told you what happened last night, didn't he?'

I nod.

'And?' says Alissa.

'And what?' I ask.

'You don't believe me, do you?'

I don't know if it's normal to feel dislike for your own daughter now and again. Sometimes Alissa is so damn superior I could slap her. It probably also has something to do with the fact that she knows me so well. Knows me and sees through me.

'Of course I believe you,' I lie.

'You don't.'

'What do you want me to do?' I ask, laughing nervously. 'Shall we get a lie detector?'

'My lie detector's in here,' says Alissa, tapping her forehead. 'That's all I need.'

'How clever of you!' I say, jokingly. 'What else do you know?'

'That you think I'm lying. That you think I'm a tart because of the way I treated Simon.'

Now I've had enough. That wiped the smile right off my face. My voice gets louder.

'I never said you—'

'Please leave me alone,' Alissa interrupts.

'But—'

'Alone,' she repeats, closing her eyes.


I feel like chucking the kettle at the wall. I could tear the kitchen apart. I could bang my head on . . .

'Well?' asks Robert.

I don't turn around. He shouldn't see my face.

'She doesn't want to talk,' I reply.

Robert comes closer and stands behind me. The kettle in my hand begins to shake.

'You should talk to each other more often,' he says, putting his arms around me.

'Good idea,' I say, pushing him aside. After I've put the kettle on the hob, I take the jam, butter and yoghurt out of the fridge, pour muesli into a bowl and slice a banana into small pieces. I manage all of this without any problem. I peel two oranges and butter some bread for Jan. When the kettle whistles, I pour water on to the tea.

'Sarah?'

'Yes?'

'Turn around, will you?'

I turn around, my face frozen, the smile embossed on it.

'What's the problem with you two?'

I want to answer that there's no problem. We're mother and daughter. We have typical mother-daughter problems. But that's a lie.

'Sometimes I hate her,' I say and I'm so relieved that the words are out that I repeat them straight away, 'Sometimes I hate her, Robert.'

He looks at me, startled, and I quickly put my hand in front of my mouth because I'm smiling with relief.

# Evelin The Best Friend

'See you later!' I call into the house, and close the door.

God, it's cold!

I pull my hat down over my ears and bury my hands in my coat. It stopped snowing in the night. The pavements are icy and the tyre tracks on the street are grooves filled with dirt.

As I turn the corner, I see Nina and forget to breathe for a moment. I knew she was coming, I just didn't know that seeing her again would take my breath away. She blushes and tries unsuccessfully to hide a parcel behind her back. I hug her much too tightly.

'Ouch!' she cries, and laughs.

I kiss her on the mouth, breathe her scent in deeply and feel the warmth under her coat. Nina.

'You must have missed me,' she says, kissing me back softly.

'How long has it been?' I ask.

'Four days.'

'Four days are a long time. Can you wait for me?'

'But—'

My lines trip out as though they're part of a rap song, 'Alissa's in a tough spot. I've got to hurry. I left you a note. It's on my desk. Here.'

I give Nina my key.

'I'll be quick, OK? Please don't go, will you?'

'I've missed you,' she says.

'*I've* missed *you*,' I say.

'I could come with you—'

'It's better if you don't.'

I hug her once more.

'And don't look under the bed. I want to be there when you open your present.'

On the underground my head won't stop spinning. I'm torn between being loyal and enjoying myself. What wouldn't I give to stay with Nina, drink tea with her and see her eyes shine when she opens my present. I hope her eyes will shine.

I haven't known Nina very long – a year maybe. And we've only been going out since the autumn break. I don't know very much about her and want to be with her all the time and learn everything about her. But I can't do that to Alissa. Not today.

After two stops I get out at *Sophie-Charlotten-Platz*.

We can't meet at Alissa's house because she's had a row with her mother. And she didn't want to come to my place because Nina was coming over. We could have met in a café, but Alissa insisted on the park.

'Is this seat free?' I ask.

She's sitting on a bench at the edge of the lake. Even though it's early, a few kids are playing around on the ice, chasing each other. Alissa looks up.

'Evelin—'

It's the second time this morning that I hug somebody. In comparison to Nina's warm embrace Alissa's is hungry and confused. I stroke her head and hear her sob. Something must really have gone wrong at her house.

'Have you got a tissue?'

I rummage around in my rucksack, find a torn Kleenex and hand it to her.

'Thanks.'

She blows her nose loudly and looks out over the ice.

'Look over there,' she says.

I can see children, two dogs, and a lonely hockey player chasing his puck. The playground on the other side of Lake Lietzen is deserted.

'Well?' I ask.

'Over there between the trees.'

I check out the trees, but there's nobody there.

'There's nobody there.'

'Look more closely.'

And then I see him.

'Oh no.'

Alissa starts to tell me how she found Simon in front of the flat this morning and put him in her bed, and how he knelt down afterwards in the kitchen to kiss her hand.

'Sarah doesn't believe me. She . . . she thinks I . . .'

More tears. Her mother makes me sick.

'. . . he's . . . Simon stood around in front of our house all morning, you know . . . and then, then he followed me here . . . I . . . I don't know what to do, Evelin. I really don't know.'

She looks at me pleadingly and I think, *This is what it looks like when somebody's giving up.* I'm just about to say something encouraging when Alissa gets to her feet. She looks over at Simon, who's leaning against a tree on the other side of the lake, and suddenly shouts:

*'Go away! Just go away! Get lost!'*

The children look over at us, the lonely hockey player forgets his puck, one of the dogs barks and Alissa stands there. Her breath comes out of her mouth in angry clouds.

'Sit back down,' I say.

*'Go away!'* Alissa screeches over the lake.

'Sit down,' I repeat, pulling her down on to the bench. Her expression is strange, her lower lip trembling.

'Hey, Alissa!'

'What?'

I cup her face in my hands.

'Calm down, please.'

'He—'

'Calm down.'

138

She swallows, she nods, and the haunted look fades from her face a little.

'Maybe I'll take that job as your bodyguard after all,' I try and joke.

'I can cope,' says Alissa without smiling. 'I just don't know where I can hide. I . . .'

She rummages around in the outside pocket of my ruck-sack, finds my cigarettes, and lights one of them.

'. . . I just have to stay outside where there are people, then I'm safe, you see?'

'Is that why we had to meet here?'

'Clever, eh?'

I wouldn't describe it as clever, more like worrying. She's getting paranoid. Smoking doesn't suit her either.

'How's this for an idea?' I say, trying to make my voice sound confident. 'We'll collect some of your things and you can stay at my place for the rest of the holidays, OK? There's enough room. You can sleep in the spare bedroom. Then we'll be next door to each other and we can sneak through the house in the middle of the night or watch telly till break-fast. What do you think?'

'But that won't solve the problem,' she says.

'We'll worry about the problem later. Simon will calm down. I really think he will. But the most important thing is you. I want you to feel better. As for your mother, I mean, do you really want to face her tomorrow at the breakfast table?'

Alissa throws the half-smoked cigarette into the snow.

'I hate smoking,' she says.

'I can understand that.'

'But what . . .' she says, looking at me finally, '. . . I mean, what will Nina say?'

'She'll be pleased. She's always wanted to meet you. And what better time than now – when you're happy and full of energy. My best friend through and through.'

I grin at her. Alissa laughs awkwardly, but I'm still pleased to see it.

'OK,' she says, 'let's do that. But . . . could we stay here a while longer and talk? I mean, just because . . .'

She knows that Nina's waiting for me.

'No problem,' I say, taking the rucksack off my shoulder. 'Have you had breakfast yet?'

Alissa shakes her head. I suggest walking up to *Kantstraße* to get some coffee and croissants.

She shakes her head again.

'I don't want to bump into him,' she says. 'As long as he's on the other side of the lake and I can see him, I'm safe. Go ahead. I'll wait here and keep the bench free.'

'Are you sure?' I ask, looking out over the ice. I don't want to leave her alone. If that loser decides to approach her, I don't want to miss my chance to castrate him.

'He won't do anything,' says Alissa. 'He knows there are too many people here.'

'That's not exactly reassuring.'

Alissa shrugs her shoulders. She probably doesn't find anything reassuring any more. A mother who doesn't believe her and an ex-boyfriend who won't let her out of his sight.

'I'll be right back,' I promise, kissing her on the cheek.

I make a quick call home from a phone box. My father answers the phone and passes it on to Nina.

'I'm bringing Alissa with me,' I tell her. 'In an hour or so. I'll explain the rest when we're there.'

I have to walk two blocks to find a bakery that's open. The croissants are still warm, the coffee is boiling hot. When did we start drinking coffee? It's really odd. At some point you start to do things that never interested you before – drinking coffee and smoking cigarettes, lighting candles during the day, sitting on the floor and answering the telephone with a Yes?

When I get back to the park, Alissa's no longer alone.

'Where did that come from?' I ask, unpacking my bag.

It's a ginger kitten. It's tiny, six months old at most. It looks quite out of place in this winter landscape. There are small lumps of ice sticking to the fur on its stomach and as I stroke its back I can feel how skinny it is.

'A stray,' says Alissa lifting it up on to her lap.

We drink our coffee and talk about everything, but not about Simon or her mother or the two figures who visited Alissa two nights ago in her room. This is time out. Alissa feeds the kitten with bits of croissant and even laughs a couple of times. And as we talk the number of strange things that have happened in the last few days finally sinks in. It all started at Christmas and since then my best friend has been swept along by it and hasn't had any peace. I hope she'll be able to find some peace at my house.

The kitten has curled up on Alissa's lap and is purring away. Alissa looks relaxed too, even though her gaze keeps wandering over to the other side of the lake.

'Why don't I go over there and tell him what I think of him?' I suggest, wiping my greasy fingers on a paper napkin.

'Better not,' she says, without looking up from her coffee.

'I really mean it.'

'I know you really mean it, so stay where you are. I'd rather you left him alone. Just now he's capable of anything. You should have seen him this morning, the way he—'

'Oh shit!'

Simon has stepped out from between the trees. It's creepy, almost as though he heard us talking about him. He stands on the path for a whole minute and looks over at us, then he starts moving and climbs down from the bank on to the ice.

My first impulse is to run for it. Stupid, but true. Then the anger comes and I think to myself, *Let him come. I'll show him! Just let him come.*

Alissa has a different reaction. It takes a few seconds for Simon's movements to register, then she jumps up, spilling her coffee and knocking the kitten off her lap. I stifle a nervous laugh. This is like slapstick comedy. The kitten emerges from the snow, startled, and looks around with an insulted expression. There's a brown patch in front of our feet where Alissa has spilt her coffee.

'Don't overreact,' I say. 'Blokes like Simon get turned on by it. Stay calm.'

'I'm sorry,' says Alissa to the kitten, bending over to pick it up again. But the kitten has had enough for one day. It jumps from one hole in the snow to the next and lands on the ice. This is a whole new experience for it. Its paws can't find any hold, it falls on its stomach and gets back up again uncertainly. As soon as it finds its feet, there's no goodbye wave or thank you. It just disappears over the ice.

'Forget it,' I say and look over at Simon. He's stopped in the middle of the lake and is looking back and forth between Alissa and the kitten. I think I can hear his thoughts. *Alissa*, he's thinking and then *kitten*, and then he starts moving. Absurdly, he follows the kitten.

'What's he doing?' asks Alissa.

I move over to her and say, 'Come on, let's go.'

'What's he doing?' Alissa says again.

'It doesn't matter. Let's go while he's distracted.'

I leave the empty cups and the napkins on the bench. Alissa doesn't move. I look out over the ice. Simon and the kitten have disappeared around a corner, we can't see them any more because of the trees.

'Come on.'

I take Alissa's arm and we turn away from the lake. Everything's fine. We'll be home soon and then we can hole up inside.

'When did we start drinking coffee?' I ask, to change the subject.

'Coffee?' asks Alissa, confused.

'Yes, coffee. I couldn't stand the stuff before. It was like—'

*'Alissa! Aaaaa-lisssssa! Aaaaaaaaa-lisssss-saaaaa!'*

The cries ring out like a siren. We don't want to stop moving. We stop. We don't want to turn around. We turn around. It's Simon, of course, yelling after Alissa. And he's holding the kitten in his outstretched arms.


He's like one of those knights who searched for the Holy Grail, so that they could give it to the lady of their heart. Even though Alissa told me what had happened in her kitchen this morning, I couldn't picture it. Not until now.

Simon comes closer. He kneels in front of Alissa and holds out the kitten. It hangs in his hands lifelessly, like a stuffed toy that's been in the washing machine once too often. Its red tongue is poking out from between its tiny white teeth. Simon smiles, Alissa takes the kitten, and I freak out.

# Alissa The Winter Child

I can't do anything. I hold the dead kitten in my hands and watch as Evelin starts hitting Simon. She forces him back and chases him out on to the ice. I can't do anything. I don't even hear what kind of insults she's hurling at him. I simply can't do anything apart from look down at the kitten.

I can feel its ribs under my fingers. Ribs like bent tooth-picks. It's lying still in my hands. I press it to my chest because I don't know what else to do. I bury my face in its wet fur, smell wetness and dirt and maybe something of the warmth that was still in its body a few minutes ago.

*It's my fault.*

*It's over.*

*Dead.*

Finally the tears come.

*What's happening here? What on earth is going on? And what's wrong with Simon?*

There are so many questions I'd like to shout out. But I keep my mouth shut and kiss the kitten's head, pressing my lips firmly against its coat and the delicate skull beneath, as though by doing so I can let it know how sorry I am.

*Why did Simon . . . ?*

'Alissa?'

Evelin's standing in front of me.

'What are you doing?'

'The kitten,' I say quietly, looking down at my hands. 'It's . . . It's dead.'

Evelin bites her lower lip, then she looks out over the ice. Simon's standing in the middle of the lake with a bloody nose. Blood runs down over his lips and drips from his chin. But he doesn't do anything about it, he just stands there without moving, his arms by his sides, waiting.

'Let's get out of here,' says Evelin.

'What about the kitten?'

'We . . .'

Evelin looks at me. I feel as though it's taking all her self-control not to knock the dead kitten out of my hands. I wouldn't even be angry with her if she did. I need somebody to tell me what to do. I feel like I'm made of straw.

'. . . we'll wrap it up in a newspaper,' continues Evelin, 'and bury it at home in the garden, OK?'

I nod. I'm glad she didn't lose her temper.

'OK,' I say, and at that very moment the kitten begins to shudder in my hands.

'Oh—'

I drop it, startled, and take a step back. The kitten's lying in the snow, it's moving, shaking and stretching. I can hear the cracking of bones. Then it lifts its head and looks at me. It straightens itself up hesitatingly, starts to move gradually and rubs its head against my leg.

'Evelin,' I say helplessly, but she's disappeared. I try to step even further back, almost falling over the park bench. I want to get away from the kitten. I know very well that it wasn't breathing. Maybe it was the fall. Maybe its heart started working again after the fall.

*That's not true. It started moving in my hands long before it fell.*

I walk around the park bench and look at the kitten following me through the deep snow. It's playful, sweet.

'Keep calm.'

Suddenly Evelin's standing next to me, holding my hand.

'Let's get out of here,' she says.

*What about the kitten?* I want to reply, but I don't say anything. The kitten has stopped moving and is watching me with its head on one side, just like Simon watched me from the ice. I recognize the similarity. Both of them are standing there, watching.

Evelin tugs at my arm and I go with her, not looking back once. What I can't see can't follow me. Evelin, however, turns round a couple of times. Only after we've left the park does she say, 'If this carries on, I'm calling the police.'

Part of me thinks that's right, and another part doesn't. I don't know why. I'm full of straw. I want to keep running away until my head is empty and I can't think any more.

'. . . because of your mum,' says Evelin.

'What?'

'Don't you want to call the police because of your mum?'

'What's this got to do with my mum?' I ask.

'She thinks you're responsible for Simon's state of mind. That he's lovesick and all the rest of it. You're doubting yourself because she doesn't believe you. It's obvious.'

I don't say anything. I don't know how Evelin came to that conclusion. She looks over her shoulder and says, 'I think we've lost him.'

The *Kaiserdamm*, usually full of traffic, is empty in both directions. It feels like a badly lit country road. The slush has a grey shimmer, and when I look up, I realize why the light is so faint – the sun has disappeared behind a bank of cloud. The longer I look out for it, the more I have the feeling that it's removed itself from our world.

'Perhaps he's had enough,' says Evelin, rubbing her right fist. Her knuckles are swollen from hitting. She says she's never done anything like that before and feels like a boxing champion.

'You're safe with me,' she says with conviction, and I believe her, I want to believe her. She puts her arm around my hips and I hold on to her tightly, as though she might disappear any minute like the sun behind the clouds.

I look back because I want to see with my own eyes that Simon isn't following us. There's nobody on the bridge that crosses over the *Kaiserdamm*. The spell is broken. *Bye, Simon.*

A shadow steals over the left lane and disappears under the cars.

'There's something there,' I say, more to myself than anybody else.

'What?'

'Back there. It disappeared under one of the cars.'

Evelin turns round. There's nothing to be seen.

'Probably a rat,' she says and we carry on.


Evelin takes the spare key out of the flowerpot while I wait on the veranda. What I saw before was no rat – I'm sure it was the kitten. Simon caught it because of me and because of me it almost died. Maybe I can make it up somehow. Maybe I can take the kitten home with me. *Jan would like it and Robert wouldn't have any objections, but Mum . . .*

I abandon that thought and ask myself where the feeling of horror came from when the kitten rubbed its head against my leg. What was that about? Why do I think I have to take care of everybody? Evelin's right. I should look after myself first. That's enough of a task.

'Did you see him?'

I shake my head. Evelin goes past me and opens the door,

while I look into the shadows and crannies of the houses one last time. The kitten remains invisible, but I still have the feeling that it can see me.

'Come on,' says Evelin, 'before you freeze on me too.'

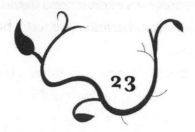

# Simon The Loving One

The blood on my face has frozen and peels off my skin like dried glue. I pick at a red strip and let it fall on to the ice. The cold has numbed the pounding in my nose. The pain is distant. I feel as though I need to sneeze all the time. Alissa and Evelin leave the park. Evelin looks back and I raise my hand and wave at her.

*Where are they going?*

I'm staying where I am. I know I can find her. Alissa knows it too – she'll lead me to her. I stand on the ice, close my eyes and think *Alissa*. I think *Alissa* a hundred times a second.

It takes a while.

A whole minute.

Then the connection is complete. I know where she's going.

I wait. I wait in front of the house. I've been waiting in front of the house for an hour and I need something to eat. I'm faint with hunger, my stomach is all cramped up. I go to the phone box on the corner. I've got a good view of the street from here. If Alissa leaves the house I'll see. I've got everything under control.

'I'd like to order a pizza.'

'Can I have your name and phone number, please?'

'I'm in a phone box.'

'And where would you like the pizza delivered?'

'Here.'

'To the phone box?'

'I'm going to eat it outside, if that's OK.'

'That's fine, but how do I know you're not messing me around?'

'Because I'm hungry, for God's sake!'

Silence.

'I'm not sure about this.'

'Hey! I'm about to starve here and I can't leave.'

He makes an exception. He tells me the pizza will be there in a quarter of an hour. It arrives eleven minutes later. I pay and rip the cardboard lid off the box. I sit opposite Evelin's house in the doorway of a doctor's surgery on the warm cardboard lid and eat the pizza with my fingers. There's no reason to hide any more.

I eat the pizza greedily. I should have ordered two. And something to drink as well. And as I'm sitting there eating, I notice something. Over there on the other side of the street. I go over. The kitten's curled up in the snow on the bottom step.

'You again,' I say. I'm surprised, because I thought the animal was dead. When I tried to catch it and bring it back to Alissa, something went wrong. I slipped and crashed on the ice. I didn't hurt myself much because I landed right on top of the kitten. I heard its bones crack and when I picked it up, it hung in my hand like a wet rag.

'What are you doing here?' I ask.

The kitten looks up. Our eyes meet.

'You too?' I say, surprised.

The kitten blinks.

'Crappy, eh?' I say and give it a corner of my last slice of pizza. Now there are two of us.

'It's me, Simon.'

'Hi. What's happening?'

'Alex, I need help.'

'Cool. What do you need?'

Alex pinched the car from his mum. It's a well-known fact that no car is safe from us and for some reason the police never pull us over. Up until now none of us has got caught. We do it properly. Forget about getting a driving licence. Who wants to wait a year when you can drive right now?

'Maybe they'll make a TV series about you,' says Alex, handing me a warm coat and a blanket, a Thermos flask and a bag of things to eat.

'What kind of a series?' I ask.

'I dunno, man. Do I look like I work for the telly or what?'

Alex looks over at the house, where the lights are warm and cosy.

'You've really lost it, man. You know that, don't you?'

'Tell me something new.'

'She's not that great.'

'Hey! Watch what you're saying.'

'Yeah, yeah.'

He pushes his mobile into my hand.

'The number of my other mobile is saved under # and then 0, OK?'

'Thanks.'

'Any time.'

He nods, looks from me to the house, and from the house back to me.

'Why are you really doing this?' he asks.

I return his gaze. Obviously, being lovesick and all the rest isn't a good enough explanation. I'd find it hard to believe myself given that it's minus thirteen degrees and there's a snowstorm on the way. Nobody's that stupid.

'You don't really want to know,' I say.

'Don't talk shit,' says Alex, hopping from one foot to the other. 'You can at least tell me that much, man. Just in case the people from the telly ask questions. Why?'

I think about it for a minute, trying to find the right words.

'Because I can't help it,' I say. 'Because I have to.'

'Because you *have to*?'

Alex sniggers and I grab him by the lapels on his jacket, pull him close and hiss into his face. 'You think this is fun? You think I've got nothing better to do than stand around in this fucking cold making an idiot of myself? *Is that what you think?'*

He shakes his head, wide-eyed. He's scared of me.

'I just can't help it,' I add quietly, breaking off eye contact. I have to let him go, quickly.

Alex disappears into his mum's car without another word. I look at the mobile. Forget it, he's no use now. After he's driven away, I put the coat on and order a second pizza. I fold the blanket into a pillow and sit down again in the doorway. Hopefully the police won't turn up. I'd give them something to think about.

# Nina The Uncertain One

There are photos on Evelin's walls. Snapshots and photo-montages and a few from passport photo machines. I feel a bit jealous. Alissa suits her. Why didn't Evelin fall in love with her? Why did she fall in love with me of all people?

Lying on Evelin's bed, I fold my arms behind my head and picture what it must be like to wake up here in the morning. With Evelin next to me.

*Good morning.*

*Good morning.*

*Did you sleep well?*

*Mmm, how about you?*

*Great.*

And then breakfast and maybe a shower . . .

I must have fallen asleep. I can't remember having heard music before. Evelin's father's nice. Her mum's always busy. When I arrived she waved briefly and disappeared into one of the rooms. Evelin's father explained that she's doing a PhD and forgets what's going on around her because she's so stressed out.

Voices and steps.

I jump up from the bed and smooth out the blanket. A quick glance in the mirror, I tuck my loose hair behind my ears and a smile like a toothpaste advert.

'Flirt,' I say to my mirror image, and leave the room.

Photos lie. Photos are tricks of time. I would never have recognized Alissa on the street. She looks older, like the big sister of the girl next to Evelin on the photos.

'I'm Nina,' I say, squeezing her hand.

'Great, now you know each other,' says Evelin, putting one arm around my waist, the other around Alissa's. We walk along the corridor to the kitchen like this. We can't fit through the door. We fool around. And then we make some tea.

'What a story!' I say, two hours later.

Now I know everything and sit there like somebody who's seen a film and wants to talk about it. But I get the feeling that neither Evelin nor Alissa want to talk about it any more.

'It sounds as though Simon is really crazy about you,' I say.

'Crazy,' says Evelin, 'is the right word.'

'I wish he'd disappear,' says Alissa.

'You mean disappear, like, *completely disappear*?'

No, of course that's not what she means. Me and my stupid questions.

'I want to be left in peace,' says Alissa. 'I just want him to leave me in peace. That's all.'

Evelin leans over and strokes Alissa's head. It looks so nice I want to do it too. Then Evelin starts to tell us how she chased Simon over the ice. I can tell straight away that Alissa doesn't want to hear about it. But then she asks in an absent-minded voice, 'Did he say anything?'

'What does it matter?' says Evelin. 'I'll make some more tea, OK?'

'Evelin, did he say anything?'

Evelin hesitates and looks at me questioningly. I nod. Alissa wants to know.

'He said he belongs to you. He . . . he said he's yours.'

'That's what he said?'

'That's what he said. About a hundred times, until I gave him another smack in the mouth. Then he shut up.'

Alissa presses both hands over her eyes. It's a strange sight. She looks like somebody who's about to lose it and is scared that her head might explode.

'Everything OK?' I ask, putting my hand on her knee.

We're sitting in a triangle on the floor, Buddha-style, then Evelin gets up to make tea. I wish she'd sit down again.

'I don't get it,' says Alissa, without lowering her hands. 'I just don't get it.'

Evelin crouches down and takes her wrist.

'It's got nothing to do with you,' she says, pulling Alissa's arms down.

'Please, open your eyes,' I say.

Alissa opens her eyes. There's not a tear in sight. Just pure anger.

We get permission from Evelin's parents to take the television into her room. Once the VCR is plugged in and we've got a bowl of nibbles each and a coke, we start watching films. At some point during the night Evelin sneaks into the kitchen and comes back with a bottle of red wine. We make a mess of the cork and eventually have to push it into the bottle because nothing else will work. I feel as though I'm drunk after my first sip. There are bits of cork swimming in my glass and I chew on them like gum. Evelin suggests dancing. Alissa rummages around in the CDs and puts on *Scott 4*. I really like it, I saw the band in concert, so I dance a bit too. Evelin and I kiss each other and Alissa claps. I like her a lot. If only her bloke would disappear.

Later Alissa says that she can't walk any more, she's too drunk. We lift her up by her arms and legs and carry her into the spare bedroom. Evelin kisses her goodnight on the cheek. So do I. Now I know her. Now we're friends.

I'm feeling really nervous as I clean my teeth. I can't look Evelin in the eye. But she talks non-stop while spitting tooth-paste in all directions. In her bedroom we open the window for a minute, put some nice music on and cuddle our way into bed. Evelin's wearing pyjamas, I'm only wearing knickers and a T-shirt, but I'm not cold. I unbutton her top and put my face on her stomach. I can hear her breathing and gurgling in there. I kiss her stomach – it's covered in sweat. Then she pulls the T-shirt over my head and caresses my body. Stars explode in front of my eyes and I have to swallow and swallow as though I'm drinking something. I find it difficult to breathe and I wish the window was open again.

'Wait,' says Evelin, getting up to open the window.

Cool air blows in. It's the special cool air that you only get in winter. I'm so happy, I want to cry.

When Evelin gets back into bed next to me, she's naked. I stroke her legs and feel the goose pimples. I'm so nervous. I want her to kiss me, I want her to hold me, I'm afraid of her. And then she kisses me, kisses my neck. I can feel her teeth on my skin – she's a vampire. If she leaves a love bite, I'll have it framed. Her mouth brushes over my ear, I can feel her tongue.

'Evelin,' I say quietly, holding her head between my hands. 'Evelin . . .'

We look into each other's eyes. This is our night, we're waiting for somebody to make the first move. We don't blink. There's so much electricity between us that the air bristles. Evelin gently presses her lips against mine. She kisses me and says my name into my mouth.

'Nina . . . my Nina . . .'

# Alissa The Winter Child

Laughter.

I'm woken up by laughter, open my eyes and close them again quickly. The room spins and my head feels as though it might detach itself from my neck at any minute and float up to the ceiling. Slowly the feeling fades. It also takes a minute for me to realize where I am. The window and the door are in the wrong place – this isn't my house. I remember Robert's dream, waking up again and again and never leaving the dream. But this isn't a dream. I'm in the spare room, Evelin and Nina are next door, and their laughter has woken me up. Now it's quiet again.

I try to read my watch in the dark. Ten past five. I realize I forgot to call my parents. Damn! I was drunk a minute ago and now I feel sober. As soon as it's light, I'll phone home.

I pull on my jumper and leave the room. There's a terrible taste in my mouth. I want to get a glass of water in the kitchen before I go back to sleep.

As I walk past Evelin's door, I press my ear against it. It's quiet in her room. I'd like to see the two of them now. Do they cuddle up face to face in their sleep? Or are they lying one behind the other?

I cross the hallway and take care not to make any noise on the tiles. In the kitchen I switch on the light above the sink and take a bottle of water out of the fridge. It feels strange being here. Even if Evelin says I should make myself at home, I find it difficult. No idea why. Maybe I haven't known her and her family long enough. Who knows what my life would be like if I'd been friends with Evelin since I was small? If she'd been there when my father died.

I put the glass into the dishwasher and turn off the light. I creep back along the hallway, take off my jumper and get back in bed. I fall asleep immediately.

And wake up bathed in sweat.

My stomach hurts and I feel as though my lungs are being squashed together. The blanket lies heavy and wet on top of me. I kick it away and get up. Or at least I try to get up, but am forced to roll back up into a ball.

*Have I got my period? I can't have, I . . .*

I manage to get to the window. Cold air, icy and reassuring. I hear myself groan and feel as though I'm burning from the inside. I breathe in the air greedily.

*What's happening to me . . . ?*

Sweat runs into my eyes, sweat runs down my back. I want

to lean out of the window and fall into the snow. I have to get outside.

*Quick!*

As I try to move away from the window, I can feel my feet sticking to the tiles. I leave wet prints behind wherever I stand. I'm not just burning, I'm melting, and then there's this pain, this awful—

*Out.*

The whole house seems to be on fire. I feel as though the walls and the furniture and everything I pass are giving off heat. I'm a magnet, I'm an overcharged battery.

*But the heat can't be coming from me – that's impossible.*

I leave the room, lean against the wall in the hallway and try to get dressed, put my bare feet into my boots, throw on my coat and—

*Faster!*

I've no idea how I manage to open the front door without making a noise. My hands are shaking, my whole body is shaking uncontrollably, and I don't know whether these are drops of sweat or tears running down my face. My blood is boiling and the pain in my stomach is murderous. Maybe I've got appendicitis. Maybe—

*Ahhhhh!*

I'm outside. I'm—

Oh God, the cold is wonderful! Pure relief. I open my coat

so that the cold can get to all of me. It's like a miracle. The pain dies away, the heat in me cowers. The night surrounds me, cold, blue and icy, and there's a quietness in the air as though time has frozen.

*Yes.*

I sit down on the top step and shake with relief. The pain is still there but only in the background. I can really feel it when I press my hand into my stomach. Resistance, as though a knife is trying to get out from inside.

*What's . . . happening . . .*

I rub snow over my forehead, I push snow into my jumper and giggle with relief. The pain has dimmed and if I carry on like this I'll be able to put it out. I push my toes against the heels of my boots and slide them off. My toes dig down into the snow.

*More!*

There's quiet all around me. It's stopped snowing and it's so early that the street lights aren't on yet. There's no light to be seen in any of the houses.

I open my mouth and drink in the frosty air. From the corner of my eye I notice a movement. I bend over – there's a dark heap lying on the bottom step. I get up and walk down the steps.

'Kitten?' I say, unsure.

The kitten is lying in a hollow in the snow. Its marble-sized eyes look at me fixedly and for a moment I'm afraid of the tiny animal.

'What are you doing here?'

I bend over to stroke the kitten on the head, when the pain in my stomach grabs me again. I double up, sink into the snow on my knees and get up again with difficulty. I manage at the second attempt. The kitten presses its head against my hand and purrs throatily. I push my finger under its belly. It licks my wrist. Its tongue is raw and icy. I sit down on the fourth step from the bottom and stretch out my other hand as well. The kitten doesn't protest when I lift it up out of its snow nest and put it on to my lap. It lies there quietly. Quiet and cold.

I feel for its heart with my fingers.

'You're . . .'

I fall silent. The kitten looks at me without moving, then makes itself comfortable on my lap and licks my hand almost thoughtfully, not like an animal that doesn't have a heartbeat.

'One day you'll just have to take us all home with you,' says a voice from the darkness.

I'm not surprised to hear it. It almost makes sense that Simon is nearby. Even if I can't explain it, I expected it. If only there wasn't this pain, then maybe I would be able to . . .

I don't know what.

My teeth are clenched. I can hear myself whimpering, rub my bare feet through the snow and try to extinguish the heat inside me.

*Pull yourself together.*

'Why are you doing this?' I ask into the darkness.

My voice croaks. I have to clear my throat so he can understand me.

'Why are you following me?'

Simon's figure peels out of the shadows. He crosses the street, wrapped up in a bulky puffer jacket and carrying a steaming cup in his hand. He stops three metres away from me in between two parked cars. He sips at the cup, pulls a face, and pours the contents out on to the street.

'Wrong question,' he says. 'You shouldn't be asking me why *I'm* doing this. I have no choice in the matter. You have to ask yourself what *you're* doing. I'm just one of those clowns playing a supporting role. And the little thing over there . . .'

He points at the kitten with his empty cup.

'. . . crossed your path by chance.'

'What are you talking about?'

'Eternal love, Alissa. Eternal faithfulness. We belong to you. Only you.'

I shake my head. Light spots dance in front of my eyes.

'Simon, I . . . It's over. Leave me alone. Please.'

And he stands there and starts to cry. Again. But this time I don't have the feeling that this is a show, like the one he put on the time we saw each other at the playground. I want to say something sensible, I want to find the right words and sort things out once and for all, when the pain begins to glow and dance around in my stomach again.

I double up and almost squash the kitten on my lap.

'Don't you think I want to leave you alone?' continues Simon, sniffing. He flings down the cup and comes closer.

'Don't you think I want to be free? I . . . I can't think about anything else, I can't do anything else. I have to be with you, have to see you, have to . . . I . . .'

He strikes a fist against his chest.

. . . 'I'm yours.'

He comes closer. The kitten is purring with pleasure in my lap. Everything around me is moving out of focus. I have to concentrate to see them clearly and I see how Simon sits down two steps below me and puts his head on my knee. Nothing else happens. He stays there, his head on my knee and his hands between his legs.

'Simon?'

No reply. His back rises and falls. He's asleep.

I nudge his shoulder. I want him to go away. I want to get up and go inside and—

*I can't go inside. I'll burn if I go inside.*

The kitten on my lap stretches and sinks its claws into my jeans. It has rubbed its back up against my stomach and closed its eyes. *Can you feel me burning?* I want to ask it, but the only thing that comes out of my mouth is glowing breath. The kitten's ears twitch briefly, then its left paw touches Simon's forehead. Sleep. The whole city is sleeping and I'm sitting here on fire.

'Evelin,' I say quietly, 'please, wake up. Please, wake up and help me, please . . .'

My eyes close, I can't hold out any longer, I don't want to. I give up and let it happen. The fire climbs out of my stomach, flows through me and burns me. It burns the kitten and Simon and then it turns to face the rest of the world.

# Part IV

# Robert The Stepfather

It's the third day and I'm still afraid. Her temperature falls in the morning and rises in the evening. A leg compress, tea, sleep and the inevitable antibiotics. I'm worried about Alissa. I'm really worried about her.

The emergency doctor explained to us that he'd never seen anything like this. No frostbite, no changes to the face, hands or feet, just heat that turned Alissa into a human radiator.

When we picked her up from Evelin's, I stood for a while on the spot where Alissa had sat overnight. The snow had melted. Two steps below I could clearly make out where her feet had been. The snow had melted there too. A layer of ice remained. I could see the red stone steps gleaming through it.

I've decided not to tell Alissa anything about this. I recognize a miracle when I see it. If I talked about it, it would be as though I doubted. I'm calm and cautious. Everything's going to be fine. Sarah's nervous though. She thinks it's her fault.

'If we hadn't argued,' she says, 'then she'd have spent the

night at home and nothing would have happened.'

I tell her that's nonsense. You can't put the clock back and think everything would have been different. Sarah isn't listening. I think her guilt makes her feel good. It gives her something to do while Alissa's ill.

The most difficult thing is preventing Evelin from spending all her time by Alissa's side. There are phone calls, surprise visits and constant questions.

She feels guilty too.

'I was asleep,' she says. 'I should have known something would happen.'

And Evelin tells us over and over again how she woke up with a strange feeling. She couldn't find Alissa in the spare room and thought she might have left already. Then the phone rang. It was the neighbour telling them they should do something about the homeless people on their doorstep. Evelin looked out and saw Alissa sitting on the steps and Simon lying at her bare feet.

'Thirsty.'

I fetch a glass of water. Alissa drinks in short, painful gulps. Her tonsils are swollen, her lips are raw and cracked. A permanent film of sweat covers her forehead. No matter how often I wipe it away, a minute later it's there again.

'Better?'

She nods, and I put the glass on the bedside table. The thermometer reads 40.3. Another day.

'It'll be better tomorrow,' I say, the way I do every day, wiping her forehead with a wet flannel and asking myself again and again how the two of them managed to fall asleep in the cold and what on earth they were doing out there.

When she wakes up she feels better at last. She eats some soup, sits up in bed and answers my questions.

'I don't know,' she says, avoiding my gaze.

'What do you mean?'

'We . . .'

She bites her lower lip. Her cheeks are almost white.

'. . . we wanted to talk and we . . . we must have fallen asleep.'

'Just like that?'

'Just like that.'

She's lying. Nobody falls asleep just like that when it's so cold. And nobody wants to talk to somebody who pushed them to the ground and stalked them. But I keep my mouth shut. I don't want to put any pressure on her – at least not as long as she's running a temperature. I look forward to hearing what Simon has to say. He was taken to hospital with hypothermia. A blood test revealed nothing. No drugs, no alcohol.

'How's he doing?' asks Alissa.

'Better. The antibiotics have kicked in and they're gradually getting him back on his feet. He had a worse time of it than you. He's got bad frostbite on his face and hands. The doctors say he's lucky to be alive.'

Alissa puts the soup on to the tray.

'But nothing happened to me?' she asks, looking at her hands.

'You were lucky.'

She puts her hands back on her stomach and says quietly, 'It wasn't my fault.'

I nod, even though I don't know whether to believe her or not.

'Of course it wasn't your fault,' I say. There are two liars in the room now.


'Where's the kitten?''

'Which kitten?' I ask.

'The tiny ginger one.'

'I haven't seen any kitten.'

'If you see it hanging around outside, will you let it in?'

'Alissa, you know what Sarah's like about pets.'

'Please,' says Alissa, closing her eyes.

Even though I know it's crazy, I keep a lookout for a ginger kitten. That same evening I see a drawer lined with a blanket next to the radiator on the floor in Alissa's room. As nobody seems to be bothered by it, I don't say anything and Alissa doesn't ask about the kitten any more.


Two days before New Year's Day there's a new development. Sarah has announced that she'd like to be left alone with

Alissa for a while. I hope something will come of it. In the afternoon I go out and do the shopping for that evening. Jan is playing at a friend's house, so I don't have to worry about him. I just have to remember to collect him later. When I get back from the shopping trip, Sarah's car has disappeared from its parking space. I go into Alissa's room.

'Well?'

She smiles at me apologetically. Words aren't necessary.

'Things will improve,' I say. I regret talking Sarah into this.

'I'm sorry,' says Alissa.

'Get better first,' I say. 'Then we'll see what we can do about the rest.'

'I'm sorry,' she repeats. 'Mum hates me.'

'Don't say that.'

'But she hates me!'

I put the shopping on the floor and put my arms around her. I'd like to talk, but I'm afraid I might start off an avalanche. I'd like to say, *Alissa, you won't forgive your mother for getting pregnant so soon after your father's death. I know you felt it was disloyal. We didn't plan it that way. It was an accident. We really didn't have a choice. And now we have Jan, surely that's a good thing? Isn't that a good thing?*

Later that evening I talk to Sarah. She raises her eyebrows and says, 'That's absolute nonsense, Robert. It's such a long time ago.'

'You're right,' I say, and think how damn difficult it is to mediate between two people who won't put their cards on the table.

# Evelin The Best Friend

'Hi.'

I stroke a damp strand of hair off her forehead. She wakes up, blinks, looks at me.

'Are you feeling better?'

Alissa shrugs her shoulders. Her face is pale. Her eyes remind me of burnt-out matches.

'I've brought you some fruit, but I expect everybody brings you fruit.'

We laugh awkwardly. It's the first time I've seen her awake. Robert tried to keep me away from her. Time out for Alissa, he called it. I think he didn't want her to be reminded of that night and everything that happened.

'What on earth happened?' I ask.

'I've got a problem,' replies Alissa, sitting up. I plump her pillow up for her and push it behind her back.

'What kind of a problem?' I ask.

She glances towards something behind me. I look over at the radiator, where there's a drawer lined with a blanket.

'That's for the kitten,' she says. 'As soon as I can, I'll let it in. I know it's waiting outside, but Mum'll freak out if I go anywhere near the front door. Simon's the same now, too.'

For a moment I'm lost, then she adds, 'He and the kitten belong to me, you see? They . . .'

'Is that why you crept out in the night?'

She shakes her head.

'I was burning,' she says. 'Here.'

She touches her stomach, then closes her eyes for a moment. When she carries on talking, her voice is expressionless.

'I've been thinking a lot about how it all happened. Can you make any sense of it? No? It sounds strange, doesn't it? And it's so complicated. I don't understand it at all yet, but I'll get to the bottom of it. Do you have any idea what I'm going on about?'

I shake my head, avoiding her gaze, and look at the drawer.

'Maybe it's best if I come back tomorrow,' I suggest. 'When you've rested and—'

'Please don't, Evelin.'

'What?'

'Please,' says Alissa, squeezing my hand, 'stay away for a while.'

'But—'

'Only for a while, OK? A few days, maybe.'

'But why?'

'Don't ask, please. We'll see each other at school.'

'That doesn't make sense, Alissa. You've been in bed for a week. This isn't the way to—'

She interrupts me sharply. 'Do you want to belong to me as well?' My hand hurts in her grasp.

'What are you talking about?'

'Look at Simon,' she says. 'Look at the kitten.'

'The kitten's dead,' I say.

'That's what I thought, too,' she says. 'It was dead and then . . . I'm sorry, I can't explain it yet. I don't know enough.'

'Alissa, I want—'

'You should go now.'

Harsh words. Direct. No compromise. Go, Evelin.

'You really mean it?' I say.

'I really mean it,' she says.

'Fine. I'll . . . I'll call you.'

'Please. Just go. I'll be in touch. Leave me alone for a while, OK?'

'How can I say no to that?' I ask with a fake laugh.

'Don't even try,' replies Alissa.

I can feel myself breaking out into a sweat – from fear, from confusion and because I'm hurt.

'OK,' I say, bending over to hug her.

Her arms stop me, her hands push hard against my chest.

'Don't,' she says.

'All right,' I say, moving away. The empty drawer in the corner of the room scares me. I turn around once more at the door. Alissa has closed her eyes and seems to be asleep.

She's sitting there like a corpse. Pale, sad, and somehow not of this world.

'Call me,' I say quietly and leave her room.

Two days later I'm at a New Year's party with Nina. People are shouting at each other and the music's too loud. I'm not in the mood for anything. The sparkling wine tastes like cat pee, the salads are limp and some guy comes over twice to talk to me. He claims he's a friend of Simon's and asks me if I'm a lesbian. The second time I put my cigarette out on his jeans and leave him sitting there with a stupid expression on his face. Shortly before midnight Nina and I decide to stop smoking and get mercilessly drunk before we start smoking again. None of it's any fun.

Four days later school starts again and it's a terrible week. I shouldn't have let Alissa push me away so easily. I think about her all the time. The days aren't the same without her around.

I lose count of the number of times I have to force myself not to call her or how often I take a different route only to end up in her street as if by chance. I never ring the bell, I never stand in front of the door, I never dial her number. I just stare at the receiver and wait for her to call.

Nina tries to distract me. Cinema, cafés, walks, love. Even though she doesn't have any answers, she believes everything will be OK.

I wish I could share her optimism.

On Thursday I've had enough and go over to Alissa's. Nobody answers my ring. I go back in the evening. Robert is surprised to see me. He doesn't ask me to come in, instead he pulls the door shut behind him and stands in the corridor in his socks.

'Sorry,' he says, making a face at the door. 'There's a bad atmosphere in here at the moment, a sort of delayed New Year depression.'

When he hears that Alissa hasn't been at school at all since the end of the holidays, he lets slip a swear word and tells me that she's been living with her grandmother since New Year's Day.

'What?' I say. I've been completely conned.

'It was her idea. I was sure she'd told you.'

'Not a word.'

This is what had happened: Alissa got better and started arguing with Sarah all the time. So when Alissa suggested moving in with Granny Netta for a while, Robert and Sarah were really relieved.

'Let's keep the school thing quiet for now, OK?' says Robert. 'If Sarah hears Alissa's been playing truant, she'll freak out. I'll go over there tomorrow lunchtime and talk to her.'

'If you like . . .' I say. I don't need to finish my sentence.

'Would you do it?' asks Robert.

It almost slipped out of me that that's what friends are for, to take care of each other. But I'm too worn out with worry to throw clichés around. So I say that of course I'll do it, tomorrow straight after school, no problem. Robert gives me the address and before I go, he makes me promise to call him at his office as soon as I've talked to Alissa. I scribble his phone number on the back of my hand and go home.

Sure enough, Alissa doesn't turn up at school the next day either. I take off after the first break because I'm too nervous to sit around uselessly for another five hours.

At *Theodor-Heuss-Platz* I catch the 194 bus travelling west towards *Staaken*. Alissa's grandma had a stroke nine months ago and had to give up all her usual activities – no delivering meals-on-wheels to pensioners any more and no more walks through the woods either. Since then she's been living with her husband Leon in a house by the water in *Pichelsdorf*.

I get out at the Lake Pichel stop and walk down to their house on *Paddlerweg*. *Heerstraße*, the main road, is behind me. After a few steps it's so quiet, it's almost as though I'm no longer in Berlin.

Leon opens the door and looks at me as if we don't know each other.

'Hello,' I say.

'I can't remember your name,' he says, laughing apologetically.

In the last three years we've only seen each other once, on

Alissa's birthday. There's no need for him to feel embarrassed that he can't remember.

'Evelin,' I say.

'Bingo,' he says, putting out his hand.

'Is Alissa in?' I ask.

'She's down by the water. Would you like to wait?'

I take off my coat and shoes in the hallway. Leon tells me that Grandma Netta is taking a nap and asks if I want to stay for lunch.

'I'd love to,' I reply.

He points upstairs.

'Alissa's staying in my old study in the attic. Just go upstairs and make yourself at home. She'll be back any minute. Would you like some tea?'

'Maybe later,' I reply, and go up the stairs.

The door to the study isn't closed properly and when I push it open the scent of bergamot hits me. The attic has two windows and both pairs of curtains are open. There's a candle holder at the end of the bed and there are piles of books lying around. There's a desk, clothes thrown over the sofa, a TV in one corner, a cat basket in the other. A bunch of dried flowers hangs from the roof beams and the wooden floor is painted white. I can tell where Alissa slept last night from the impression she left in the bed.

I sit down on the sofa and wait. While I'm waiting I try to find Alissa in the little things – in the books, the discarded clothes and the bunch of dried flowers. I don't succeed. I can't find any real connection between this room and Alissa.

'I'll go and look for her,' I say.

Leon is standing in the kitchen, peeling potatoes. He dries his hands and walks me to the door.

'Look by the jetty,' he says. 'Sometimes she walks as far as the edge of the woods to get a better view over the River Havel. You really can't miss her. As soon as you come back, I'll make some tea.'

'Great,' I say, pulling my hat down over my ears.

Lake Pichel, which is bisected by the River Havel, is completely frozen over and reflects the sky. A kindergarten group is walking hand in hand over the ice and somebody's dog is chasing a tennis ball. The picture reminds me of that day on Lake Lietzen when I gave Simon a bloody nose. I don't know whether he's still in hospital or not and I find myself looking for him on the opposite bank.

*Stop it.*

Alissa comes towards me a few minutes later. Behind her I can see the ice shimmering on the main body of the Havel, a few seagulls and a man feeding them. The *Teufelsberg* looms in the distance. I raise my hand and wave. She doesn't react, though I'm sure she must have seen me. I stop walking and ask myself what I'll do if she sends me away again.

Suddenly Alissa runs towards me and throws her arms around me.

'At last!' she says into my ear.

We hold each other tight for a long time and I swallow back tears. I have no idea why I feel so vulnerable.

'I'm really glad you're here,' she says, as though we'd arranged to meet and I'm late.

I can't think what to say. I grin and hug her tightly, but there are no words. We turn back towards the house hand in hand. It feels as though we haven't seen each other in years. A long journey, an exile, a new life. My head is empty. I steal a glance at Alissa.

She's thinner and the shadows under her eyes have disappeared. Her lips are cracked from the cold, her hair looks as though it hasn't been washed, and when she speaks, her voice has a strange, scratched quality.

'Will you stay with me for the weekend?' she says.

A strange noise comes out of my mouth.

'There's no need to cry,' says Alissa and stops to wipe my tears away.


First we drink tea, then we have lunch with Leon and Grandma Netta.

In the short period between meeting Alissa by the Havel and getting back to the house with her, we haven't spoken. There's a comfortable silence between us that doesn't change during the meal. Grandma Netta tells us about the new 'meals-on-wheels' kitchen she wants to open soon. Leon says he doesn't think much of the idea. Grandma Netta should be taking it easy.

Alissa keeps winking at me from across the table and at one point she kicks me gently in the shin and rolls her eyes, as though there's something very strange about all this. When she goes into the kitchen to get some mineral water, Leon leans over to me and says, 'We don't know what the matter is either.'

I'm relieved in spite of myself that I'm not the only one who finds Alissa difficult. Grandma Netta bites her lower lip, but before she can say anything, Alissa comes back and sits down at the table again.

'It's going to be really cold tomorrow,' says Grandma Netta.

'I love the cold,' says Alissa, winking at me.

After we've washed up I call my parents and tell them where I am and that I won't be coming home until Monday after school. Alissa makes tea while I talk. I carry the tray of cups and biscuits up to the attic. She follows with a blanket and a cushion.

'We can share the bed,' she says, lighting some candles. After putting a CD on, she falls on to the sofa. I sit on one of the chairs. Everything is as it always was. Alissa and me.

'I'm so glad you're here,' she says again.

I sip my tea, try to meet her gaze, look away. My questions are so stupid. They're all about my hurt feelings. And I don't want to reproach her.

'You probably want to know what happened,' she asks finally.

I'm so relieved that she's the one who's brought it up that I can only spout nonsense.

'No, actually,' I say, laughing.

'I needed to be alone,' continues Alissa, without reacting to my joke. 'I really needed it. Grandma Netta and Leon know that. Grandma Netta sent a letter to school. I'm going to stay here for the weekend, then I'm going back.'

With these words she gets up from the sofa. She goes over to one of the windows and opens it. I immediately feel the cold blowing in and moving through the room, and lift my legs up on to the chair. The candles begin to flicker, the door clicks shut. Alissa leans her arms on the window sill and looks out. Silent. I wait. This is starting to get creepy. *Hello*, I want to say, *I'm still here*. Before I can say anything Alissa starts to speak, but I don't feel as though she's talking to me.

'I wanted to sort things out in my head – you know, see everything clearly. That was the most important thing. That night outside, I was . . . there was a fire inside me and I had to put it out . . . I don't know what would have happened otherwise. It was the cold, you know. It saved me, and now – now everything's OK again. I can feel it. I've become much sharper since then. I don't miss a thing, Evelin. That's why I see them everywhere now. I can finally see them properly. There are usually two of them, and they're so careful that you're lucky if you catch sight of them. But I look closely. I . . .'

She's silent for a moment as though she's trying to remember, then she continues, 'I noticed them in town, you know, the first time. I was surprised. You can't imagine how surprised I was. I followed them straight away. But it didn't work. I kept losing them. They don't leave any traces behind, that's their secret, you know, that's how Elia and Aren disappeared. That was their secret. But I saw through it. Soon I knew what to look for and I came all the way out here. Now the River Havel is the only thing separating me from them. Somewhere over there is the way forward. I'll find the answer, I will. It's funny. I mean, it could be pure coincidence that Grandma Netta and Leon live here, couldn't it? And if anybody can understand all this, then it's you. You have to look really closely. That's why I see them more and more often. I keep coming across them and watching how they disappear and come back and disappear again. I'll find out where they go. That's why I'm here, Evelin. That's the only reason.'

Silence.

'Quick! Come here!' she calls to me suddenly.

'What—?'

'Come here quick, Evelin!'

I jump up from the chair and run to her side. She puts one arm around me and points out of the window.

'Can you see?'

I can see a thin thread of grey cloud, a few fir trees, the glow of the sun.

'Look!'

188

A raven separates itself from one of the treetops and disappears silently over the stretch of water in front of the house.

'They're everywhere,' says Alissa, looking at me contentedly. 'Simply everywhere.'

How am I supposed to respond to all this? You can't have a normal conversation with her. What I'd really like to do is shout at her and slap her face, but I don't dare. What am I supposed to say to her? Anything I could possibly say would be wrong because it all leads back to the same question: What's the matter with you, Alissa? What on earth has happened? I try nonetheless and mumble something about school. Alissa dismisses the subject and says there'll be time for that later. So I ask about her mother, and what happened between them. She laughs and tells me that's a stupid question. At last I get to Simon. Success.

'He'll be here soon,' answers Alissa. 'I can feel it. He'll find his way here. But that's OK, I'm not afraid of him any more, you see.'

'Why should he come here?' I ask.

'Because he can't help it. The kitten found its way here as well. It's only now that I understand everything, but back then, you know, when it started, it was pure chaos.'

She taps her index finger against her lips as though she's asking me to speak more quietly.

'That's why Simon will come, the same way the kitten

came. Do you understand?'

I don't understand anything. I feel my hands shaking as she tells me about the kiss that Simon forced on her.

'That was his mistake,' she says. 'That's how it started.'

'With a kiss?' I ask.

'Do you remember how I held the dead kitten in my hands and kissed its head?' she asks.

I recall the scene immediately. I even know what I was thinking at that moment – *Sick, that's sick.*

'Well, that was my mistake,' says Alissa. 'But how was I supposed to know?'

'You mean—'

'I brought the kitten back to life, Evelin. That's why it's following me everywhere.'

'That's nonsense,' I say, thinking about the little kitten's corpse that I buried in the snow before we left the park.

'Why is it nonsense?' she asks. 'You don't know the kitten. If it could, it would follow me everywhere, but it's actually much too cold out there for such a small animal.'

Alissa laughs and looks over at the cat basket in the corner of the room. I follow her gaze. I'd give anything to see what she's seeing.

'Alissa?'

'Yes?'

'The kitten . . .'

'Yes?'

I shake my head. I just can't say *Sorry, but there's nothing there*. I'm a coward, I'm too much of a coward and I'm afraid of hurting my friend. Telling her that I can't see anything would be like telling her she's gone crazy.

'Nothing,' I say instead.


I can't get to sleep. I listen to Alissa's breathing as though something might happen at any moment.

*Is this schizophrenia?*

Her face is relaxed, she looks terribly normal. I smell her, trying to find a difference. She smells normal, she still smells like Alissa.

*Are these delusions?*

As I watch her, I remember that I completely forgot to call Robert, even though I remembered to call my parents. Great.

I get out of bed quietly and creep downstairs. A clock is ticking, wind is blowing around the house. I stand in front of the phone in the hallway, hesitating. It's a few minutes past three. Who should I call? Who can I call at this time? And what on earth could I tell them?

I leave the hallway again and go back to the attic. As I'm about to lie down, my gaze falls on the cat basket. I crouch down in front of it and move my hand over the empty blanket.

*Nothing, absolutely nothing.*

In bed I stare at the beams on the roof. Alissa is sleeping deeply. I lie awake next to her until dawn and ask myself how ill my best friend really is.

## Simon The Loving One

The cold has changed or else I feel it differently.

I prefer the first theory.

I look at my hands in their thick woollen gloves. On my left hand, where the little finger and the index finger should be, the woollen fingers bend inwards. Empty. That's why my mum wants to sue the hospital.

'This is unbelievable!' she shouted at the doctor. 'We're living in the new millennium. Nobody loses two fingers just because of frostbite. I'll sue over this!'

I kept myself out of the discussion. I really couldn't care less. I don't blame the doctors. I wouldn't even be bothered if they'd amputated my hand. These things are of superficial importance.

*Alissa.*

I light another cigarette and watch the entrance to the school. The cold has changed. It's more familiar to me. Now I also know why it's so biting. I understand it. We know each other. The cold is bundled rage. Rage and longing. All in one.

I look up at the sky. A little bit of snow is falling. It'd be nice if it snowed. The cold and I.

*Alissa.*

It's not only the cold that's changed – something's happened to me as well. I can see a lot more. Where before there was chaos, now every thought makes sense. It's reassuring when life has a single focus. And you don't have to fight it. Now I understand.

*Alissa.*

I don't need to look at my watch because I know the bell will ring any minute now. For four days I've been standing here at the end of school. I know her timetable off by heart. No one can fool me. I drop my half-smoked cigarette into the snow and wait for it to go out. The smoke rises up in a thin line and disappears, the bell rings.

In the quiet that follows not much happens, then windows are closed on the top floors and shortly afterwards the doors open downstairs. I straighten up and feel how the cold has reached the sensitive spot in my armpits. It's a brief moment of perfection.

*Alissa.*

Evelin leaves the school alone. She waits at the school gate. A girl goes over to her and they greet each other with a kiss. Lesbians. Martin was right, they're lesbians. No skin off my nose. I wait. Alissa doesn't come. I keep waiting. The school-yard empties out. I take my gloves off and drop them in the snow. The cold laughs. Evelin walks to the underground station with the girl. And there's still no sign of Alissa.

*Alissa.*


In my dreams I touch her. Again and again. Sometimes I cry with longing. She hasn't answered the phone for days. It's only ever Robert. Or Sarah. And sometimes little Jan. And I hang up. I leave home early in the morning and look for her in supermarkets, cafés, parks. I watch and wait. Even at night I do my rounds. First I stop by Alissa's – the light in her room is never on. I walk by Evelin's – the light there is always on. I creep behind the house, through the garden and along the balcony. I look through the windows. Kitchen, living room, bathroom. Mum, dad and daughter. Sometimes the other lesbian is there, but there's no sign of Alissa. One day after another, I'm not giving up, I'll find her.

Even though I'm dressed warmly, the cold sticks to me. It's especially bad at night. Warmth shuns me, cold is my new friend. At first it hurt, but now I feel as though the heat of the flat is suffocating me. I hope I'm not ill with flu or one of those new viruses.

*Alissa.*


The next day Evelin disappears. She doesn't come out of school and the windows in her room remain unlit. I go home. Friday turns into Saturday. My instincts tell me that Alissa can't be far away. I feel her presence, I keep thinking I can see her out of the corner of my eye, but as soon as I look she disappears. Think. I have to think properly. I used to be able to do that.

*Alissa.*

I wander through the city. Maybe I'll find a trace of her, maybe I'll find a clue and suddenly find myself standing in front of her. People don't talk and when I ask them a question they avoid my gaze. Even my mates are strange. They haven't got any time, they're too busy and they don't understand me. I wish I knew where Evelin's little tart lives. I'm sure Evelin is with Alissa and the little tart definitely knows where that is. I keep looking. I'm not giving up. And so Saturday turns into Sunday.

From early on Sunday until the evening I walk through our area and keep a lookout. I feed myself on doner kebabs and coke, with the occasional burger. I fart non-stop and there's a crappy taste in my mouth. I'm only wearing a T-shirt under my leather jacket, anything else is too warm. I think about cornering Alissa's mother or her stepfather. A few threats wouldn't hurt. But knowing my luck, they'd call the police straight away or kick me out on my arse. I'm not healthy enough to put myself through that. The cold exhausts me. I can hardly get out of bed in the morning. The cold and my stupid penis.

In my dreams not only do I touch Alissa, but she touches me too and I wake up bathed in sweat. My body's crying out for her, every cell is singing her name. I can hear it in the silence.

*Alissa.*

Sunday night turns into Monday morning and I creep through the flat naked and stand on the balcony. If my parents catch me now I'm in deep shit. It's two o'clock, my testicles contract in the icy wind, the tips of my fingers start to hurt pleasantly. This is good. The firm snow under my naked feet reminds me of a carpet. The cold creeps up my calves and spreads into every cell of my body. I close my eyes and stretch . . .

*Alissa?*

. . . and I can feel her. Suddenly, she's there. So near. When I open my eyes, I see threads spinning through the night towards me. It's like being on a crazy trip. The threads are as thin as a wisp and glow red. They're flying towards me from all directions and when I see them I know she's thinking about me.

Right now.

*Alissa.*

# Evelin The Best Friend

I'm woken by the smell of hot toast. Alissa is sitting on the floor wrapped in a blanket and has spread our breakfast out around her. I grin when I see her. She looks refreshingly normal. She looks the way I know her: My best friend, eating toast and grapefruit on a winter's morning, drinking tea and reading a book.

'What are you reading?' I ask.

She looks up, surprised.

'Hey, you're awake already.'

'Awake is the wrong word.'

'Hungry?'

'That's more like it.'

I get out of bed and look at the book.

'Poetry?'

'Leon lent it to me,' says Alissa, pouring tea into a bowl. 'I haven't got room in my head for anything bigger than poetry.'

I flick through the book. Richard Brautigan. The poems are

short. I skim through one of them and laugh.

'Which one is it?' asks Alissa.

'One for us,' I say, reading it to her.

> *Two guys get out of a car.*
> *They stand beside it. They*
> *don't know what else to do.*

Alissa doesn't laugh. She mutters something about not under-standing it, passes me the bowl full of tea and asks how I slept. The moment has vanished. A minute ago we were Alissa and Evelin, the way everybody knows us. Now we're Alissa and Evelin separated by something that Evelin can't describe and Alissa can't explain.

That's if it *can* be explained.

'When you've had breakfast,' says Alissa, 'we'll go for a walk.'

I nod and drink some of my tea. It would have been nicer if she'd phrased the sentence as a question, but I'm up for anything. My plan remains unchanged. After this weekend my best friend is going back to her old life, no matter what it takes.

'How long do you plan on staying here?' I ask, as we leave the house.

'I'm coming with you on Monday,' says Alissa, putting her arm though mine.

'Really?'

'Really.'

I screw up my eyes. The wind is biting and blows through my clothes, stealing warmth directly from my skin. But it's a beautiful day despite the cold. The light is clear and occasionally the sun breaks through the blanket of cloud, lighting up the snowy landscape. I can feel my heart racing. I don't want to show Alissa how pleased I am that she's coming with me on Monday. I don't want her to see how confused I really am.

We walk towards the River Havel. Alissa doesn't waste a single glance on the fir trees that surround us on all sides. She's busy searching the sky. Even though I haven't said anything, she reassures me, 'They'll come, don't worry.'

We reach the end of the stretch of land. The Havel lies in front of us. The river is frozen over as far as a hundred metres in from the bank. Seagulls stand motionless on the ice, seagulls sit on the water. There are more people out walking than there were yesterday. A Saturday in Berlin.

We circle the tip of the stretch of land before turning home. There isn't much to talk about. Alissa's still searching the sky and I stare down at the ground and ask myself what I should do. The silence weighs down on me. I'm unsure and afraid of saying the wrong thing. At the same time I'm afraid of not doing enough. I'm in a terrible dilemma. This is my best friend and it's time that I admit we're circling in two different orbits.

\*   \*   \*

The day passes in a haze, every conversation leading to a dead end.

Alissa takes a nap in the afternoon. I flick through some magazines and start to read a book, drink tea and wait for her to wake up. I phoned Robert earlier and told him that Alissa was fine and that we were going to school together on Monday. What will happen after that? Will she abandon her belief in mysterious people and invisible cats or . . . ?

I shut my book. I have no idea what I've been reading for the last few minutes. The image of an institution and tranquillisers haunts my head. I'm forced to think of *One Flew Over The Cuckoo's Nest* and *Betty Blue*.

'Have I been asleep for a long time?'

Alissa looks at me. In the twilight and with the candles she's like someone from a time long past. She also looks calm. The haunted expression has disappeared from her eyes. It could all have been just a dream. Awake.

'Two hours,' I say.

'Oh.'

She sits up and yawns. I go over to the window to open it. As if they've been waiting, Grandma Netta calls up that the meal is ready. The timing is perfect. We go downstairs and eat. We chat for a while, then we put our coats on and go back out into the cold. When we come back there's tea and biscuits. We chat and listen to music, then we put our coats on again and go out for the last time that day, come back and eat and chat.

The day takes its course and finishes in front of the telly. This time I'm the one who falls asleep before midnight. It's a strange feeling. Somebody has erased twenty-four hours of my life.

The next morning begins just like Saturday. I feel as though I'm stuck in a loop. At some point the books will all have been read, there'll be no more tea left in the tea caddy, no food in the fridge. At some point we'll have to leave Grandma Netta and Leon's little house and return to reality. A cut through the loop. Tomorrow.

During our walk I talk about Nina, because I can't think of anything better. I do it for myself too, to be nearer to Nina. Sometimes Alissa's arm brushes mine, as we walk along the bank of Lake Pichel towards the main body of the River Havel. When we've walked through the wood once, we turn around and everything begins again.

'I feel old,' I say at one point.

'That's boredom,' says Alissa.

'Doesn't that bother you?'

'Not much.'

We keep walking, waiting for something to happen that will end this calm. And when it happens, I'm so startled I almost wet myself.

It's a scream.

'Quick!' says Alissa, racing off.

Through the narrow gaps in the fir trees we can see out

over the icy Pichel. A small group of people has collected in the middle of the lake.

'Wait.'

To my surprise, Alissa doesn't run out on to the ice but walks along the bank until she's standing opposite the people.

'There!' she cries enthusiastically, seizing my arm. 'There!'

At that very moment the sun breaks through the clouds and illuminates the scene with a glaring light. I'm forced to squint a little, I'm so dazzled.

'There!' cries Alissa.

'It's OK,' I calm her.

The group of people is about fifty metres away from us. A boy has fallen through the ice. I can see his head and his hands. He's clinging to the edge of the ice. The people keep well away. They probably don't want to risk a second person falling in. They've tied scarves together and thrown them to the boy. But he's too afraid to take his hands away from the edge of the ice. None of the encouraging words help and the knotted scarves lie uselessly in front of him.

'Can you see her?' asks Alissa and laughs.

She's like a child, her face glowing, her eyes huge in her face.

'She's one of them,' says Alissa. 'Isn't it beautiful?'

A dog barks. It runs around the hole in the ice and then towards the boy. It starts to skid and lands in the water with a loud splash. A second later it's disappeared under the ice.

A man tries to go after it and is held back by two other people.

'Watch,' says Alissa. 'Watch carefully.'

The boy pushes himself up on to the edge of the ice and tries to climb out of the hole. The people encourage him, then he heaves himself out completely and crawls out of the water. Like a seal he slithers over to the people stretching out their arms to welcome him.

'Yes!'

Alissa turns to me.

'Now do you believe me?' she asks and cups my face in her hand.

'You have to believe me now,' she says, laughing.

'Alissa,' I say, as the people wrap the boy in a coat and lead him away from the ice. 'Alissa,' I say quietly, 'what did you see?'

She looks at me doubtfully.

'What did you see?' I persist.

'What did *you* see?' she replies.

'I saw a boy climbing out of a hole in the ice, nothing more.'

Alissa's childlike joy vanishes. She turns pale and the sunlight makes her hair appear translucent.

'Say that again,' she asks me.

'The boy climbed out of the hole in the ice,' I say. 'What did *you* see?'

'The truth,' answers Alissa quietly, emphasizing every word. 'I saw the truth.'

30

The woman starts to get undressed. She stands on the bank of the lake and peels off her coat. Then she spreads it out on the snow and sits down. She unfastens her boots, puts them next to each other in the snow and places her socks inside. She puts her trousers, jumper, T-shirt and knickers on top of the coat. Naked, she turns away from the bank and goes out on to the ice. Her skin is like marble. She takes cautious steps. The lake is covered in a fine layer of snow, the ice beneath it polished by the wind. As the woman nears the hole, the sun comes out from between the clouds. She crouches down and covers the last few metres to the hole on her hands and knees. Although she's very careful, the ice just in front of her collapses and she slides into the water.

The boy doesn't notice her. He's holding on to the edge of the ice in panic. His lips are blue and the chattering of his teeth can be heard clearly. A group of adults and children are standing at a safe distance. They have tied scarves together and thrown them to the boy, but either he lacks the strength or he's afraid to let go of the edge. Nobody dares to go any closer – there are cracks all around the hole. The people move back. It's too dangerous.

A playful dog barks at the boy. It runs towards the hole and starts to slide, falls into the water and is sucked under the ice by the current. A man calls out. The boy is unaware of all of this. He's drifting in and out of consciousness. He probably knows instinctively that he'll be dragged down by the current if he lets go of the edge.

The woman swims towards the boy with calm strokes. She pushes her hands under his armpits and holds him like this above the water. She feels him relax and speaks into his ear. Then she lifts him higher. The boy reaches forward and in the next moment he has crawled out of the ice. The group of people welcome the boy, wrap him up in their coats and run with him towards the bank.

The woman remains behind alone and tries to get out of the water. The ice breaks and she falls back in. Only when she tries another spot does she manage to get out of the lake.

On the bank she dries herself off with her T-shirt before getting dressed again. When she looks back, the temperature and the cold wind have formed a fine layer of ice over the hole. In half an hour only the uneven surface will show that a boy fell through the ice here.

A cry rings out.

From the opposite bank of the lake a girl is running towards the woman. Another girl is following her. The woman hesitates for a few seconds before crouching down. Then she rises up from the ground and flies up over the ice. The waving girl is left behind below her. She stands still and cranes back her head.

*'Wait!'* she cries. *'Please wait!'*

But the woman doesn't wait.

# Evelin The Best Friend

*'Why won't you wait, damn it?!'*

Alissa has cupped her hands around her mouth. I can see the veins standing out in her neck.

'Alissa?'

I touch her arm. She lowers her hands.

'Is everything OK?' I ask.

'Did you see her?' she asks me.

I look into the clouds. The sky is empty. There's nothing to see.

'You didn't see her,' says Alissa.

'Who?' I ask.

'The woman. There was a woman.'

I shake my head.

'All I saw was . . .'

'. . . a raven,' Alissa finishes my sentence for me. 'Right?'

I nod and wait for her to get angry again. I can cope with anger. If she would only shout at me the way she just shouted out over the ice, then we might get somewhere. But what I see now is pure disappointment.

'Forget it,' she says, walking past me back to the bank. I follow at a distance of a few metres and catch her up. How am I supposed to react to such nonsense? Shall I pretend just so she gets her way? She'd see through me immediately and then what?

'You have to understand,' says Alissa, standing still, 'that wasn't the first time.'

'OK,' I say and she grabs my arm. She wants me to understand. She doesn't let go of my arm while she speaks.

'Sometimes I feel as though I've been watching them forever. But it's only been a week. Only a week, Evelin.'

Suddenly she laughs.

'What is it?' I ask.

'I'm sorry.'

She lets go of me.

'You must think I'm totally crazy.'

I'm silent. I can't reply. Alissa's mouth forms a hard line.

'I'm not crazy,' she says.

'I didn't say you were.'

'But you thought it.'

'That's not true.'

'What *do* you think then?'

'I think . . . I need to know more to understand,' I bluster. 'Tell me who they are.'

'What?'

'Who do you want to find, Alissa? Who are they?'

'You know that,' she replies. 'Elia and Aren and all the others.'

'Yes, but who are they exactly?' I continue. 'Who are Elia and Aren and all the others?'

She shakes her head as though I'm too stupid to understand her.

'I don't know. Did you think I knew?'

'But—'

'All I know . . .' she continues, '. . . is that they're real and they help. Not everybody. I haven't found out how they decide yet, but I'm on their trail. That's why I'm living with Grandma Netta and Leon. When they turn into ravens . . .'

'Alissa?'

'. . . I lose track of them. It's like a fairy tale. Only I don't know whether they're really ravens, you see? It's really difficult to say because it could be that they—'

'Alissa!'

I grab her by the shoulders and say, 'Be quiet.'

She falls silent.

'This is all too much for me,' I say, being very careful not to shout at her. 'I . . . I have to think about all this, OK? Can we talk about what exactly it was you saw later? Let's . . . let's go back now and talk about something completely different. Just for a while, OK?'

'No,' she says.

'Please, Alissa.'

'I want to sort this out *now*. You don't believe a word, admit it.'

'This has nothing to do with believing,' I say.

'What then?' she asks.

'. . .'

'What then, Evelin?'

'I don't know.'

'Do you want to believe me?'

'Of course I do. Why do you think—'

'If you want to believe me, give me another chance, OK? Just one more.'

'And what happens then?' I ask.

I still have my hands on Alissa's shoulders. She grabs my wrists and squeezes them.

'Then you'll understand me,' she replies, without really answering my question.

Twenty minutes later we go back out into the cold.

I put the rucksack with the thermos flask and the sandwiches on my back. Leon is standing in the corridor, looking at me sceptically.

'I'm worried,' he says.

'Me too,' I admit.

'She's been up on the *Teufelsberg* a lot and I worry every single time. Here, take this with you.'

He goes over to the coatstand and takes a mobile phone out of his pocket.

'There's a sticker on the back with our phone number on it. Promise me you'll call if you need help.'

I nod, steps sound from the attic, Alissa comes down the stairs, I stick the phone into my coat.

'Ready?' she asks.

Her face is glowing. She's holding a tube of cream in her hand.

'Otherwise our faces will freeze off,' she says.

I stand still while Alissa puts the cream on my face, then she disappears into the living room for a second to say good-bye to her grandma. When she comes out, the purposeful-ness has disappeared from her eyes for a moment. I can see that she's sad and I can imagine what's going through her head. Since she had her stroke Grandma Netta sleeps all the time and talks about plans that she can't carry out any more. That's hard for Alissa. She always idolized Grandma Netta.

'Everything OK?' I ask.

'Great,' she says, trying to smile back at me.

We promise Leon that we'll be home in time for dinner, then Alissa takes me by the hand, the door falls shut and the winter has us in its grasp once again.

We travel three stops on the 194 bus back in the direction of town and get out at the *Postfenn* stop. It's windy and cold and not a day for climbing a mountain.

'If only it were a mountain,' says Alissa.

We look like we did on Christmas night, when we were

searching for her father's grave – woolly hats, boots, and eyes screwed up against the cold. Only the heavy snowfall is missing. And my motivation, of course.

'How many rubbish dumps can there be that have turned into mountains like the *Teufelsberg*?' I say.

'That's the wrong question,' answers Alissa. 'You should be asking how many mountains there are that are actually rubbish dumps.'

'The Himalayas,' I say.

'Mount Everest,' she says.

We can't think of anything else to say on the topic.

A couple, well wrapped up, come towards us. They're the last people we meet on the way up to the top. I don't know what kind of mood you have to be in to walk up here on a day like this. Nature fans can cope with anything. As, apparently, can girls who have sworn each other eternal friendship.

'Do you remember when we were up here with Jan last autumn flying kites?'

Alissa keeps walking as though she hasn't heard me.

'Was that last autumn?' she says after a few metres.

'That was last autumn,' I say.

Alissa stops walking and puts her head back as though she can see the kites in the sky.

'I came up here with Simon as well,' she says.

'Oh.'

'At night once,' she says.

'Was . . .'

I don't want to put my foot in it. I don't want to rub her up the wrong way, and I definitely don't want her to think . . . Stop it. That's enough. I'm not her babysitter, she's not ill, I don't want her to be ill.

'Was probably lovely,' I finish my sentence.

'It was great,' she says, looking at me. 'You should have been there. Millions of stars and a totally cloudless sky. Everything was still OK back then.'

She smiles and stretches out her hand towards me. We continue on our walk side by side.

The view from the *Teufelsberg* is grey and depressing. It's too early in the day to see the city lights. I feel as though I've come to the end of a difficult climb.

'I'm too old for this,' I say, collapsing on to a park bench. 'Let me lie down here.'

'Not there. That's the wrong side,' says Alissa and keeps walking.

I follow her on to the south-west face. We clear the snow off one of the benches and sit down. At last! When my breathing has calmed down a little, I take the thermos flask out of the rucksack and share a cup with Alissa. We don't say a word. The wind blows around us on all sides. Now and again it flings a shower of hailstones in our faces.

'How idyllic,' I say.

'But the view's good,' says Alissa, taking a jumper out of her rucksack. There's a case inside the jumper and inside the case there's a pair of binoculars. She gets up, puts the binoculars to her eyes and searches the area. She knows what she's doing – I would probably have held the things the wrong way round. She checks out the surrounding area for two whole minutes. I sip on my tea and wait to see what will happen next. At last she hands me the binoculars.

'Try and find the Grunewald tower,' she says, pointing towards the river.

I stand next to her, feel her warmth on the plastic of the binoculars and see a blurry landscape. When I've adjusted the focus properly, the Grunewald tower appears before me.

'OK, I've got it.'

'Tell me what you see.'

'The tower, trees, snow, ice, water . . .'

'Then wait a moment.'

Minutes go by and I get impatient, shifting my weight from one foot to the other. I'm slowly starting to get a headache from the terrible cold.

'I can't see anything,' I say, slightly irritated.

'Just one more minute, Evelin.'

One minute, a second minute.

'Now,' says Alissa.

*How can you see something when I don't see it, even though I've got a stupid pair of binoculars in front of my eyes?* I want to ask her, but I keep my mouth shut and don't move from the spot. Only when my eyes start to water do I lower the binoculars.

'Was that it?' I ask, doubtfully.

'The longer you look, the more there are.'

'There were two ravens, Alissa.'

'I know. We have to wait a bit longer.'

*What for, Alissa?*

If this was anybody else but her, I'd have been in the bus and on my way home a long time ago. I'll do anything to save my best friend, so I raise the binoculars and wait patiently.

Over the next hour I count twenty-one ravens flying either to or from the south-west, spreading themselves out over Berlin. When Alissa begins to talk, at first I think she's talking about the ravens.

'I've been watching them for a week – that's how I discovered them in the first place. I noticed them on the street. There was this man. He sat down next to a girl who was waiting at a bus stop. She was alone, staring at nothing, and he put his hand on her shoulder. The girl didn't look at him and when he took his hand off her shoulder, she got up and walked away from the bus stop. I ran up and spoke to the man. He was really surprised and you can imagine how surprised I was too when he crouched down and turned into a raven. Have you noticed how many ravens there are in Berlin? I even took the lift to the top of the television tower to look at them. That brought me here. That's why I'm living with Grandma Netta and Leon. It's only a stone's throw away from here and this is the best place, I'm telling you. I'd really like to go up the

Grunewald tower too, but I don't think that's allowed.

I lower the binoculars. My eyes are watering from staring for so long and my head's splitting.

'So what do you think?' Alissa asks me.

'I don't understand,' I say. What I mean is that I don't understand what she's talking about. A hand on a shoulder and turning into a raven? I bite my lower lip. *Please, Alissa, wake up.*

'But now you know there's something there,' she says.

'Ravens,' I say.

'A lot of them.'

'It's winter, Alissa. Ravens always turn up in cities in winter. Ravens, crows, magpies.'

'And the woman?'

'What . . . which woman?'

Alissa tears the binoculars out of my hands.

'You don't *want* to see them,' she says angrily. 'That's your problem.'

'Wrong,' I say. 'My problem is, I *can't* see them. How am I supposed to believe that a man can turn into a raven when I can't see it?'

She smiles.

'So you think it could be true and that I can see them even though nobody else can?'

Silent. Our eyes lock together and I say softly, 'I don't know what to believe, Alissa. I'm sorry. And even if I did believe, what difference would it make?'

'I'd have an ally,' she says.

'An ally. What for?' I ask.

'To help me track them down. I want to know where they come from. That's all I want.'

I can't look her in the eyes any longer. I'm not her ally.

'One day,' says Alissa, gazing out towards the tower, 'I'll follow them. Then I'll find out where they come from and I'll show you.'

'You'll need wings for that,' I say.

'Maybe I'll grow some.'

'Maybe you will,' I say, and the wind dies down for a second as though it wants to keep hold of my words. At that very moment it begins to snow again.

We pack our things and turn towards home. My thoughts are spinning. OK, there were a lot of ravens and I'll admit that it's strange that they all flew in the same direction but what does that prove? I'm not an ornithologist. I can't throw specialist terms around and explain the behavioural habits of birds. I can only understand what I see. And I saw birds, nothing but birds.


'Is Robert picking you up?' Leon asks me, after he's locked the door. We've eaten and washed up. Even though it's only nine o'clock, I'm exhausted and just want to collapse in to bed.

'No, we're taking the bus.'

'Good,' says Leon, and we go into the living room to say goodbye to Grandma Netta. She's never awake before ten in the morning. We have to leave here at seven to get to school in time for the first lesson.

'It was lovely to have you here for a few days,' says Grandma Netta. 'Sometimes it's so quiet, I feel as though Leon and I are the only people on the planet.'

'Don't worry,' says Alissa, 'you're not.'

'Guaranteed,' I promise.

'That's reassuring,' says Leon and laughs.

Alissa and I lie in bed next to each other in silence. We've said everything there is to say and I'm too tired to find out more about her visions. I just want to fall asleep and wake up and go back to the real world. I want to put my arms around Nina, see my parents, and not worry about Alissa any more. With that thought I fall asleep.

A noise wakes me.

One moment I'm in a deep sleep, the next I'm wide awake and sitting up straight. Alissa isn't lying next to me. I expect to see her at the window or sitting on the sofa with her legs drawn up to her chest, lit up by a candle. The attic is dark, nobody is sitting on the sofa or standing in front of the window. There's only Alissa's bag waiting by the door, ready to leave.

'Alissa?'

I get out of bed and go down the stairs barefoot. There's no light on out here either. I look into the kitchen and the bathroom. Even though I know she's not in the living room, I look in there for a moment.

'Alissa?'

Only then does it occur to me to look in the hallway.

Alissa's boots are missing and her coat isn't hanging on its hook. I run up the stairs in the dark. I have to get dressed. If I hurry, I can catch up with her, wherever she's going. If I hurry, then—

A cold wind blows around me.

'Nice nightdress,' says a voice.

My head turns to the left, where one of the windows is open.

'Wrong direction,' says the voice.

I look to the right and there he is, sitting in the dark, one leg crossed over the other.

'Where there's one, there's another, I thought to myself. But the other one seems to be hiding.'

'I don't know where she is,' I say automatically and hear how shaky my voice sounds. It's not as though I'm afraid of him, but it's not as though I'm pleased he's turned up here either.

'Such a pretty liar,' says Simon, geting up from the sofa.

'Simon, I—'

'No, don't say anything. Wait and listen to what I've got to say first.'

In a few steps he's standing next to me and grabs me by the throat. His fingers are icy.

'OK, let's try again. Where's Alissa?'

He pushes me back against the door until it closes. He shoves his face into mine.

'I'm not interested in you,' he says and in the half-light I can see the dark patches left by the frostbite on his chin and cheeks.

'You're simply not important.'

'Thanks,' I croak, and suddenly I can't breathe. Me and my stupid mouth. Simon has lifted me several centimetres off the floor.

'Shh!' he says.

'Simon—'

'Shh!'

He grabs hold of my arm with his other hand and pulls me away from the door. I wait for my anger to kick in. Two weeks ago I chased this bloke over a frozen lake and gave him a bloody nose. Today I'm one of those hopeless victims who put up with everything in the hope that it'll soon be over.

We sit down on the sofa. His left arm moves around the back of my neck, his right hand remains at my throat.

'This is exactly how we're going to wait,' he says, making himself comfortable.

I can feel myself separating from my body, observing the two of us from the outside. A sado-masochistic couple sitting on a sofa in the middle of the night, he with one arm laid tenderly around her, just as tenderly he presses a hand to her throat. She sits next to him in her nightshirt and knickers, as passive as a lamb to the slaughter. What a crappy role.

'How long have the two of you been hiding out here?' asks Simon. 'No, you don't have to tell me. Since Friday, right? On Friday you disappeared from home, right? Was Alissa waiting for you here?'

He taps a finger against his nose.

'You're surprised, aren't you? It's all instinct. My instincts led me out here. It doesn't matter what Alissa does, I'll always find her.'

'What do you think you're doing here?' I ask.

'Nice try,' he says, stretching his legs.

'If you weren't a lesbian,' he continues, 'I'd teach you a few tricks. But as it is, I have to decline.'

He laughs.

'I'm really looking forward to her. She hasn't revealed all her secrets, she hasn't told me about all the things she can do. Do you know what I'm going to do when I find her? I'm going to crawl inside her to get really close. I'll find the deepest point in her, and that's where I'm going to stay. I want to feel how she feels from the inside. I want to hide away inside her. That has to be the way, don't you think? You can't imagine how much I'm looking forward to it.'

'You're sick,' I say.

He laughs, then he points towards the door.

'What's that?'

Before I can react, he's on his feet and is bending over Alissa's bag.

'That's my—'

'Shut up!'

He undoes the zip and rummages through the clothes.

'This isn't yours.'

He buries his face in one of the jumpers.

'No, this is definitely not yours.'

He looks at me.

'She was here and she'll come back, right? And you don't want to tell me where she's gone, correct?'

I think I can hear his brain working, then he laughs and says, 'Hold on, hold on, let's try again. You don't actually know where she is, right? You woke up and she was . . . she was . . . gone! Am I right? But she's not been gone long, I can smell that she was here a short while ago. She must have sensed I was coming. My little Alissa.'

With these words he rushes out of the attic. Just like that. I can hear him on the steps. The next moment the door downstairs bangs shut and I can move again at last.

# Part V

**32**

The loving one doesn't notice the stairs under his feet. He runs down them, not touching the floor once as he rushes along the hallway. The air around him takes a step back, space opens up for him.

In front of the house the loving one stands still and looks around.

*Where?*

He turns his head, he lifts his face towards the night.

*Alissa.*

He breathes in deeply and then follows the winter child out on to the ice.

It's because she's so close – it's because she's so close that it's easy for the loving one to keep on her trail. There's a connection between them that fades and dies at a distance. Get closer, however, and the connection is made and increases in intensity. The loving one can feel it throughout his body. He knows what the winter child is thinking. More importantly, he has finally realized what she really is. A door. A bridge. And he also knows what she's doing out here in the night.

She's searching.

*For me.*

*Who else?*

*Yes.*

The loving one begins to run.

Soon he can see the bright surface of the River Havel through the trees. There are two dark spots on the ice moving away from the bank.

*She isn't alone. Who's with her?*

The loving one stands on the bank for a minute and looks out over the ice. The winter child is being followed by what looks like a giant fish. It reminds the loving one of films about the Arctic – the hunter travelling, the hunter at one with nature.

*Wherever she's going, it's time for us to meet.*

*Now.*

The loving one jumps on to the ice.

'Alissa!' he cries. 'Alissa, I'm coming!'

There's the night and the river. There's the ice and the wind blowing the snow before it, pushing it into sharply angular ramparts at the river's edge. Cold, stormy, not a night to be outside. The moon is hiding, the sky looks torn, the stars flicker out of focus and far away the roar of the motorway can be heard.

There's the night and the river and the winter child running over the ice. She's pulling a canoe on a rope. The canoe has been stolen from a shed by the jetty. It slides behind the winter child and threatens to overtake her whenever she pulls on the rope. Just before the winter child reaches the border between ice and water, she hears a cry. She turns around and sees a ghost – a pale face with a gaping laugh.

*Oh no!* thinks the winter child. She cannot move from the spot.

The loving one slows down. He knows the winter child cannot escape him this time and curses himself for losing a night . . .

He no longer knows how long ago it was. His memory is in chaos and the winter child is calling to him out of the chaos.

'Alissa,' says the loving one, breathless, coming to a stop in front of her.

Now that he's close he can see it isn't a fish but a canoe. He laughs. The boat is a two-seater, under ten metres long, 60 centimetres wide at most.

'You won't get very far in that,' says the loving one.

'I don't want to get very far,' replies the winter child.

The loving one stretches out his hand.

'I won't go with you, Simon.'

'You have to. I need you.'

'Simon . . .'

'I can see them,' says the loving one. 'I see the craziest things. I see birds turn into people and I see people turn into birds. They appear out of nowhere and then they disappear again over the city. *I see them everywhere.* And all thanks to you, all—'

'You . . . you can see them?' the winter child interrupts him.

The loving one laughs.

'As if you didn't know.'

He shakes his head.

'As if you hadn't known for a long time already. That's why I need you, that's why you call for me. You're my gate, Alissa, I can see them through you. You have to help me and turn me into one of them.'

'I'm sorry, Simon. I don't know how.'

The loving one shakes his head regretfully.

'Don't worry. I'll give you time. I've got all the time in the world. I've been looking for you for days. I stood outside your school and waited for you. I kept watch outside your house and followed your best friend. What do a few more days matter? The important thing is that you led me here. Come with me now. I'll hide you in my room and feed you and take care of you. I'll love you forever and creep inside you as deep as I can. We can do that for as long as it takes for you to let me in, do you hear? Until I'm one of them. Come on, nobody will find out.'

The winter child lowers her gaze. When she speaks, her words are just a murmur.

'. . . I didn't want any of this . . .'

The loving one can't believe his ears. The wind is creaking and groaning over the ice, the fir trees are whispering. No, the loving one must have heard wrong.

'You didn't want this?' he asks. 'You really mean you didn't want this?'

'Simon, I . . .'

The winter child falls silent. They look at each other, then the loving one laughs and says, 'As if it made any difference! As if what you wanted made a single shitty bit of difference. You . . .'

He tips his head to one side.

'What are you doing out here then? You . . .'

He comes a step closer.

'You're on your way to them. That's it, isn't it?'

The winter child steps back, but the loving one is faster. In two quick steps he's standing in front of the winter child and clasping her face in his hands.

'Ah, if you only knew how happy I am to be so close to you!'

The loving one leans forward and kisses the winter child. His eyes roll behind their closed lids, his mouth trembles. He kisses the winter child again and licks her lips.

*'That's enough!'*

The winter child pushes him away. The loving one reels,

his eyes are shining and he feels as though he's lost his sense of balance. When he comes to his senses, he is no longer the boy he was a few seconds ago.

'I hunger for you,' he says with a calm voice and moves closer again.

The winter child reaches into the canoe and lashes out with one of the paddles. The loving one catches the blow effortlessly and throws the paddle behind him.

'Is that all?' he asks, forcing the winter child back step by step, away from the boat, further out on to the lake, close to the border between the ice and the water.

'Where are you going?' he asks. 'Where can you go now?'

They come to a standstill at the same time and the loving one stretches out his arms.

'Come to me,' he says. 'Come, let's make the journey together.'

The paddle hits the back of his neck with a slap. The blow throws the loving one forwards. He falls right in front of the winter child with arms outstretched and lands hard on the ice. His hands move for a moment, then he lies still.

They look at each other for a long time, both breathless, then the winter child says, 'Thank you.'

'You're welcome,' replies the best friend.

She hurriedly pulled on jeans and a jumper. She followed the loving one out of the house in such a panic that she didn't have time for socks or a coat. Her feet are bare and cold in her boots. She's shivering from head to toe.

'You'll freeze if you stand around here any longer,' says the winter child.

'I'm not going back without you.'

'Evelin, I've waited far too long already. I have to find them.'

'By creeping off secretly in the middle of the night?'

'You would never have let me go.'

The best friend flings the paddle down on to the ice.

'Of course I wouldn't have let you go. Nobody would have let you go. Isn't that obvious? I don't understand you, Alissa. I thought we didn't have any secrets and then you sneak off just like that. I should be grateful to that loser over there because without him I'd never have found you.'

The best friend kicks the canoe.

'What were you going to do? Did you plan on sailing round on the River Havel until those mysterious strangers pulled you on to dry land?'

'Something like that.'

'Meaning?'

The winter child points down the Havel.

'I know they're out there somewhere. I can feel it. You saw it yourself, they flew in that direction.'

'In that direction could mean anything,' says the best friend. 'You could search for days on end.'

'I don't think so.'

'She doesn't think so,' repeats the best friend and for the first time you can hear the fear behind her words.

'Do you know what, Alissa?' she says, rubbing her arms. 'Do you know you're driving me absolutely crazy? I . . . I could slap you, I could . . .'

The best friend runs out of words. The winter child says, 'It'll be over soon.'

'And what happens then . . . ?'

'. . . then I'll be Alissa again. Believe me.'

The best friend avoids Alissa's gaze. She doesn't believe it. Then she points to the loving one.

'What are we going to do with him?'

'We can't leave him lying here,' says the winter child. 'He won't survive another night in the cold.'

The best friend shrugs her shoulders.

'As far as I'm concerned we can push him into the water. At least then he's guaranteed not to turn up again unexpectedly. I'm sick of his little stalker act.'

The winter child laughs.

'You could never do that.'

'Try me. You'd be surprised.'

Fifteen minutes later they've dragged the loving one over the ice into the house. They lie him on the sofa in the living room, close the door and stand in the hallway.

'Please, stay here,' says the best friend.

The winter child shakes her head. She thinks that if she stays now, she won't set out on the quest again. She's taken the first step. The canoe is waiting. It's tonight or never.

'Can't I change your mind?' asks the best friend.

'Not even a little,' replies the winter child.

'Then will you at least take my scarf with you? As a good luck charm?'

The best friend is concerned, the winter child feels guilty. She wants to apologize for all her tricks and lies, but before she can say anything, the best friend says, 'The scarf's upstairs. Just give me a minute, OK?'

'OK.'

'You won't run away?'

'I won't run away.'

'If you do, I'll wake Simon up and the whole thing will start all over again. Not even a bloodhound could find you faster.'

'Very funny. I'll wait in front of the house.'

The best friend takes longer than a minute to put on socks and another jumper. When she finally comes downstairs in her coat and scarf and closes the door behind her, the winter child opens her mouth.

'Shut your mouth,' says the best friend, 'otherwise you'll start spitting ice cubes.'

'You—'

'You and me. Are you really so surprised? I thought you knew me. Here's the scarf. And now let's go before I change my mind,' says the best friend, linking arms with the winter child.

# 33

# Alissa The Winter Child

It's the wind's fault. These aren't real tears, even though I could cry with gratitude. I knew that Evelin was important to me, but I didn't know how important. Until now I saw us as friends. Always together, always having fun, always there for each other. But I never counted on this. When we got back from the *Teufelsberg*, I realized this didn't make sense. Evelin simply can't see them. As far as she's concerned I'm talking nonsense. And now this. She's coming with me.

'What exactly did you have in mind?' she asks, tapping the tip of her boot against the canoe.

Now isn't the time to be honest. My plan was simply to sail down the Havel in the canoe and hope to discover the ravens' trail.

'My plan was—'

'Oh, come off it!' Evelin interrupts me. 'You didn't have a plan.'

'Didn't I?' I say, surprised.

'Don't pretend. Just tell me how we get this canoe into the

water without capsizing it. I don't plan on getting wet. Where on earth did you get this thing anyway?'

As we push the boat off the ice and into the water, I tell Evelin about the boat club.

'I pulled it out from under the tarpaulin. It was really easy.' Evelin laughs.

'No wonder,' she says. 'Nobody expects their canoe to get stolen in winter.'

'I'm going to take it back.'

'How noble of you. Are you getting in first?'

I climb in clumsily, grateful that Evelin is holding the canoe steady. I would never have managed by myself. It's a miracle that the edge of the ice doesn't break. Evelin follows me and sits down, then we look at each other and laugh.

'I'll get it,' she says, getting out of the boat again to fetch the paddle.

'Good job it didn't break,' I say.

'Good job I followed Simon,' says Evelin.

'Good job I was so slow,' I say, 'otherwise he'd never have found me.'

'And good job you're keeping your mouth shut and paddling.' Evelin taps the back of my head with her hand, but I can hardly feel it through my woolly hat. Then I push the boat away from the ice, and we glide out into the dark river.

Once we've passed the Grunewald tower, the conversation dies down. It's simply too cold to talk. Every few minutes we take turns paddling and swear when pieces of ice crash against the bow, making the canoe wobble. Then suddenly the moon comes out from behind the clouds and the river turns into a silver ribbon.

'Beautiful, isn't it?' I say.

'Fantastic,' answers Evelin.

Moving forward is difficult. I thought we'd be driven along by the current. I hadn't counted on there being so much ice to block the way.

'It would have been easier to walk,' says Evelin.

I want to tell her that walking would definitely not have been easier, but I expect she can work that one out for herself. If the ravens fly overhead and land on one of the Havel's banks, it would be embarrassing to find ourselves on the wrong side. The canoe's ideal, even if it's slow. Time isn't our problem.

'My turn.'

I hand the paddle back to Evelin and look up at the sky. There are no ravens in sight. Even the moon has disappeared without a trace.

*Soon.*


'What happens when you find them?'

'You believe me then?' I say, surprised.

'That's not the point. I'm sitting in this damn canoe with you, so give me an answer. What are you going to do then?'

'Nothing.'

'Nothing?'

'I . . . I want to find them and ask them what all their appearing and disappearing is about. That's all I want,' I lie.

'That sounds stupid,' says Evelin.

'So?' I say and hear Evelin laughing behind me.

'Why are you laughing?'

'Because I can't believe I'm paddling along the Havel when it's minus fifteen degrees outside just to hear you say *So?*'

'Cool, eh?' I say.

'Really cool,' says Evelin.

Ten minutes later the Havel widens and we get to the part of the river known as *Schwanenwerder*. I know the course of the river as if I've travelled it a thousand times. When I first discovered the ravens' flight, I began to study a map of the city. I traced the Havel with my finger on the map and tried to guess where the ravens were flying. We're still on the right track. The Havel will soon branch off, with one of its branches coming to a dead end in Lake Jungfern. Then we'll have to improvise because I don't know where the water goes from there.

Evelin hands me the paddle, then I can feel her pressing herself against me from behind, putting her arms around my waist. It's difficult to paddle like that but I don't say anything because her closeness and warmth do me good.

We reach open water and we can't see the riverbank any more in the darkness. I steer the canoe in the direction of Pfauen Island, which lies at the centre of the river. I wait for it to emerge in front of me at any moment when I hear a beating of wings over our heads.

'Wait.'

I draw the paddle into the boat, stop breathing, put my head back, keep quiet. There's no movement in the darkness above me but I can hear the beating of wings.

I narrow my eyes so that I can see more clearly.

*Please, show yourselves.*

And then they fly over our heads. Five, six, seven shadows fly over the canoe and disappear into the darkness.

*Where?*

I'm confused. I've lost my sense of direction. I turn my head frantically.

*Where did they go?*

'Left,' says Evelin.

*Left? But that's the wrong direction. That's . . . I thought . . .*

It doesn't matter what I thought, we're on their trail.

'They're flying over that lake over there, the *Grosser Wannsee*,' I say, putting the paddle back into the water to steer the canoe away from the island.


The paddle is getting lighter and there's less ice. The current picks up. A few pieces of ice still scrape against the canoe, otherwise we float along with the current, unhindered. I lie the paddle across my lap and only correct our course now and again. The night is so quiet that you would never think we were in Berlin. It's still dark and there's not a hint of morning in sight.

We sail past a jetty and a lonely night light appears, a colourless spot in the snowy landscape. Then the current drives us on and the darkness closes in again. I try my best to stay awake. I would never have thought you could get tired in cold like this. Falling asleep now would be unbelievably stupid.

When I hear the beating of wings I'm ready for it, head back, eyes open wide. The clouds in front of the moon disappear and I can clearly see the figures of two ravens above us.

We're on the right track.


Half an hour later lights peel out of the darkness and take on the shape of a villa. The ground floor is completely lit up, the first two floors and the attic have a few bright windows.

*Yes!*

I steer the canoe to the bank, but can't find a jetty. A low wall separates the lake from the grounds. I paddle as close as I can. The canoe scrapes against the wall and comes to a stop.

'Evelin?'

I don't know why I'm whispering. I feel as though I have to do everything as secretly as possible so that this brightly lit place doesn't vanish. It's my proof for Evelin. I pull at her arm which is hanging loosely around my hips.

'Evelin?'

'What . . . ?'

Her voice sounds sleepy. I can feel her sitting up behind me.

'We're here,' I say.

'Where?'

'There, behind the stone wall. A villa, a proper villa.'

'We'll never get over there,' says Evelin, yawning.

She's right, the stone wall is too high for us to climb it from the canoe. I steer alongside it and reach a wire fence. The fence ends in some undergrowth by the riverbank and that's where I run the canoe aground.

'Last stop,' says Evelin.


If getting into the canoe wasn't a problem, getting out is a different matter. One of Evelin's legs sinks into the water up to the knee and when I try to do better, the canoe capsizes and floats there like a dead fish, belly up and shiny.

'Great,' I say.

'I've got to move,' says Evelin, 'otherwise my leg will freeze.'

When she suddenly starts to giggle and runs around in a circle a couple of times, I'm surprised. She drags her leg behind her and groans.

'What are you laughing at?' she asks, limping towards me. I put the canoe between us. Evelin shakes a fist at me, then, with some effort, we pull the canoe out of the water and drag it a few metres into the undergrowth.

'What now?'

'We have to get past that,' I say, pointing to the fence.

We lift the fence up easily and duck down underneath it. We emerge on the other side between a dense row of trees. A snowy lawn borders the trees, at the end of which stands the villa. I can hear voices and want to dance for joy.

*They're here. They're all here.*

'How do you know this is the right place?' asks Evelin, after we've looked at the villa from behind one of the trees.

I look at her. Her face tells me everything.

'Intuition,' I lie, because I don't want to discuss the wide open villa doors, I don't want to talk about the light flooding out of the windows and spreading like spilt milk over the night blue snow. And I especially don't want to hear her opinions about the people sitting on the terrace – people who look like paper cuts-outs against the back-lighting. So I point to the most obvious thing, the only thing Evelin can understand.

'Look at the roof,' I say.

Evelin lifts her head, her mouth forms an O.

'That can't be a coincidence,' I say.

There are eleven ravens sitting in a straight line on the roof. They're like guards looking out over the lake.

'Is that enough proof?' I ask.

'Proof of what?' says Evelin.

\* \* \*

We skirt around the terrace sheltered by the trees and reach the front of the villa. I've got a few scruples about walking up to the brightly lit terrace. I'm afraid of doing the wrong thing. I've no idea what could go wrong, but I don't want to walk over just like that and say *Hi*. Something tells me it would be inappropriate. I prefer to approach from the entrance and ring the bell like a visitor.

'It doesn't look as though they get a lot of visitors here,' says Evelin. 'I think you can save yourself the trouble of ringing the bell.'

Two paths lead up to the front of the villa. The building looks much more compact from this side. High windows and an enormous front door. We stop right in front of it.

'Spooky,' says Evelin.

'Are you scared?' I ask.

'You're not scared. Why should I be scared?'

'I *am* scared.'

'Great.'

She points to the door.

'What do you want to do now? I told you, they haven't even got a bell.'

I raise my hand and knock. We wait. I knock again. The noise is deep and loud. Evelin leans forward and turns the doorknob. There's a clicking sound and the next moment the door swings inwards.

'After you,' she says, letting me go first.

# Evelin The Best Friend

Before my eyes can get used to the darkness, I notice the smell. Autumn. Leaves. Chestnuts. The smell of a frosty morning, misty lawns, cold without any wind. It also smells a bit like a cellar and apples in storage.

The entrance hall takes on a shape as the moon comes out from behind the clouds. Broken pieces of furniture are piled up one on top of the other and two giant bags of rubbish are leaning against them. To the left and right flights of stairs lead upwards. The banisters are missing in several places. The whole place is so run down, it's like a vision of the apocalypse. The end of days.

'Must have been a fancy villa at one time,' I say and I can see my breath escaping from my mouth like a ghost.

Alissa doesn't react. She takes a step forward and turns around slowly on the spot with outstretched arms.

'Isn't this wonderful?' she asks.

'If you're into horror,' I reply, laughing. 'Then it's magnificent.'

'Just look at the paintings,' she tells me.

In the darkness I can only just make out that there is something hanging on the wall. I go nearer. A gold frame, spiders' webs, and in between a mixture of colours. I don't know how Alissa can see it at all.

'Let's go up here,' she says.

'Wait.'

Alissa doesn't wait. It's almost as if she's high. She runs up the left-hand staircase. I follow her up the creaking stairs, expecting them to give way at any minute, dropping me into the cellar. At the top she opens the double doors and a quiet *Oh!* escapes her lips. There's a long room in front of us. It's brighter in here than it is in the entrance hall. All of the windows are lit up by moonshine, eight windows reaching up to the roof. There are leaves on the floor, leaves that have collected around the furniture, which is covered in dust sheets; leaves piled up in the corners as though they're trying to climb up the walls. I can see how the leaves got in. Two of the windows are broken. Amazingly none of the snow has blown in, but in its place there's a whole lot of dust covering the floor. It rises like mist as Alissa crosses the room. She comes to a halt in front of a dirt-encrusted fireplace. A round table with one leg missing is leaning against the wall next to it. It's a miracle there are no rats in here. I have never seen such a sad place. Patches of wallpaper are peeling off and the ceiling is a mess – cracks and holes and wet patches on the stucco.

'Alissa, we should clear off before somebody finds us here,'

I say, without wanting to. I know it's nonsense. No policeman is going to look in here by chance. But it's OK to spout nonsense, especially after I've knocked out a bloke using a paddle and stolen a canoe with my best friend so that we could sail down the half-frozen River Havel in the middle of the night. Even though I know nobody will catch us here, I want to go. Alissa was wrong. It's time for her to admit it.

'Oh, that's nice!'

Alissa is stretching out her hands towards the dark fireplace.

'What are you doing?' I ask.

'Getting warm,' says Alissa, looking at me over her shoulder. And as she looks at me, I almost believe I can see a fire reflected on her skin for a second, bathing her face in a red glow. Then the second passes and she's standing in front of a dirty fireplace, looking as though she's having a great time.

'Come on, don't tease me,' I say. 'It must be the wrong house. We should be glad it hasn't collapsed on top of us.'

Alissa turns back to the fire.

'This is the right place,' she says.

I go nearer.

'There's no fire here. What are you doing?'

'Can't you feel it?' she asks me.

I crouch down in front of the fireplace, put my hands in the ashes and show Alissa my dirty fingers.

'I can't feel anything,' I say, getting back up.

'Poor Evelin!' she says, sounding ironic, and I have the

stupid feeling that she's making fun of me. She comes over and puts her hands on my face. They're boiling hot. I pull my head away and take a step back.

'Are you making fun of me?' I ask.

'I'm not making fun of you.'

'But . . .'

Alissa inclines her head.

'Are . . . are they here?' I ask quietly.

She looks past me and allows her gaze to wander through the room.

'Are they here, Alissa?'

'They're here,' she says.

I turn around.

The dilapidated room, the moonlight, the broken window panes, autumn inside, winter outside, leaves and dust, snow and ice. Nothing has changed.

'Why can't I see them?' I ask.

'Why can't she see you?' says Alissa to the room.

Silence. What else? Only my nervous breathing and the wind behind the windows. Then she sighs and says, 'They say you don't have the gift.'

'That's it?'

'That's it.'

'Which gift?'

'The gift of seeing them . . .'

Alissa puts her hand on her stomach.

'. . . the plant.'

'So you didn't vomit it up,' I say.

'Apparently not,' she says, and suddenly she smiles.

Her smile is like a curtain lifting and I see what's been going on in her head all this time. She's glad that the plant is still inside her. She knew it the whole time.

'It might be best if you wait outside,' she says.

I shake my head.

'Please, Evelin. You're in the way.'

'Forget it. I'm not leaving you alone in here.'

'I'm safe here.'

'I—'

'Please,' she interrupts me.

'OK.'

I spread out my arms.

'But first tell me what you see.'

'Evelin, I—'

'What can you see?'

She looks past me again with her head tipped on one side, listening, then she nods, points to the windows and says, 'The curtains are dark blue and probably made of velvet – I can't tell in this candlelight. There's a sofa in front of each window, two chairs and a small table. The sofa on the far left is still free. I'd like to sit there when you've gone.'

She looks down at the floor.

'The carpet is moss green without a pattern. I didn't know it was possible to weave such an enormous carpet.'

She looks at me.

'Do you want to hear more? There are wrought iron candle holders in the corners of the room. The candles are white and there are four in each holder. There are paintings of landscapes on the walls and next to the fireplace there's a samovar on a round table. That's all.'

'And how many of them are here?' I ask.

'Is that so important?'

'It's important to me.'

Alissa looks into the empty room.

'Fourteen,' she says, taking off her coat. Beads of sweat have formed on her forehead. Even I am suddenly boiling hot. *Fourteen.*

'OK,' I say quietly. 'I'll wait outside.'

As I reach the double doors at the end of the room, I'm absolutely determined not to turn around, but I can't resist the temptation.

Behind me stands the empty room, the weak moonlight on the dead leaves, dust in the air and Alissa – coat over one arm, calm personified.

'See you later,' I say, closing the doors behind me. I stand still and put my ear to the wood.

I can't hear anything.

I wait.

Nothing at all.

*Fourteen, and I didn't see a single one of them! Curtains at the windows, a moss green carpet on the floor, a fire in the fireplace, candles, a samovar . . .*

Out in front of the villa I take off my gloves and sit down on them so that my bum doesn't freeze. Below me is the snowy pathway that rises up from the road in a curve on the left and leads back down to the road on the right. In between there's a large weeping willow. I thought they only grew close to water. I can't see any tracks on the path – our boot prints are the only things that leave a clear outline in the snow. They lead up to the entrance in an irregular zigzag pattern. I sit down on the top step in front of them and wait.

*Crazy! This is all crazy. How could I leave her alone? What's wrong with me? Now I'm encouraging her.*

I close my eyes. I don't really know what to do. I believe her and I don't. I want and I don't want to believe her, and imagine Alissa never being able to leave her fantasy world, seeing things that don't exist on every street corner. What then? How long will she be able to move between these two worlds? How long will that be OK?

*When will she lose patience with me because I can't see? When?*

For a brief moment I consider bursting into the rundown villa like an idiot and pulling Alissa out by her hair. Nobody will stop me because what I can't see can't hold me back. I'll cover her from head to toe in snow until she wakes up and everything is as it was before. Shock therapy.

Luckily moments like this are brief and soon fade.

*But it would be better than sitting around here doing nothing.*

*Anything would be better.*

I straighten my hat and try to snuggle down even deeper into my coat. I'm glad I'm not wearing a watch. I stick my hands under my armpits and think about Alissa and Simon. I picture them secretly going to the *Teufelsberg* last year in autumn to lie in the grass and watch the stars. Then I remember the night in front of our house. How did they survive that? Why didn't Alissa call me and what were the two of them thinking? I probably shouldn't have thought about that, because then I hear a telephone ringing. Right below my heart.

# Alissa The Winter Child

'Sit down,' says Aren.

Elia comes back from the samovar and hands me a cup.

'Thank you,' I say. I can smell cinnamon and orange. The tea is a dark red colour. I hold the cup with both hands and lean back on the sofa. I try to look as relaxed as possible. I can feel myself shaking in my shoes. When I look around I can see that nobody's looking at us. A few of them are deep in conversation, others are reading or just sitting there drinking tea.

As if I'm not here.

Elia and Aren pull up chairs. Aren has crossed his legs and folded his hands in his lap, but Elia is leaning forward, elbows on his knees, fingertips touching. He looks as though he might jump up at any moment. I wait for him to bombard me with questions, but it's Aren who says, 'It wasn't necessary for you to come here.'

I almost start laughing. It's a long time since I heard such a load of nonsense.

'It was *very* necessary,' I say. 'If you only knew how necessary it was, then you wouldn't be sitting here so comfortably. Don't you think you owe me an explanation?'

'There's no point in this,' says Aren, shaking his head. He starts to get up, but Elia takes hold of his arm.

'Wait,' he says.

Aren sits down again and Elia turns to me. 'We're sorry it turned out like this. If you'd fallen through the snow a night later, then none of this would have happened, but . . .'

He shrugs his shoulders and adds apologetically, '. . . it's all quite complicated.'

'I'm not stupid,' I say.

'I know. I . . .'

He looks at Aren. Aren looks out of one of the windows.

'What you saw down there in the crypt, Alissa . . .' continues Elia, '. . . was very unusual. It's not normal for a gift to be that strong. Not at all.'

'What exactly *is* the gift?' I ask.

'It's best if I start at the beginning,' answers Elia, starting to explain. As he's speaking, I sit there, but I don't hear the sentences properly. My head is running along two tracks. On one track I take in his words, on the other I feel as though I've heard them once already. They're like the soundtrack to a film that used to be silent and now has the sound added in.

Elia explains that every person is born with a gift. If this gift grows, then it brings forth talents. The manner in which the gift is treated determines how it develops. It's the old principle of talent. If nothing is done with it then nothing becomes of it.

'If the gift withers, however,' says Elia, 'then your talents wither as well. When you become an adult, the gift disappears completely. It never got that far with the dead boy. His gift hadn't developed yet. If a child dies with an undeveloped gift, it remains in its body and sometimes it tries to get out. Like a . . .'

He searches for the right word, and before he can say it, I think it.

*Seed.*

'. . . like a seed that wants to grow,' says Elia. 'You saw it yourself.'

I nod and see it before me again – the fragile plant growing out of the dead boy's chest, possessing enough strength to bore its way through the wooden lid of the coffin.

*And enough strength to make me swallow it.*

*Yes.*

Elia carries on. 'And in many cases—'

'In many cases,' Aren interrupts him, without looking away from the window, 'this seed dies. It dies with the child and the gift dissolves into nothing.'

Aren turns to Elia, 'That was one of the reasons why I didn't think we needed to talk to her.'

'But you sensed—'

'The gift *could* have withered afterwards. Inside her, Elia. It was possible.'

Elia shakes his head, lowers his eyes, and says quietly, 'You talk as though she's not here.'

Aren looks at me and I feel as though he's not real. He's far away and it's a cardboard cut-out sitting in the chair. But as he looks at me he seems to come closer, then suddenly his gaze is friendly and he apologizes.

'It isn't good to draw somebody into our world without a reason. That's why I didn't see the need to tell you everything. I misjudged the situation. Forgive me.'

I don't know whether to believe him. He's like a person waving with one hand while making a fist with the other.

'But what does all this mean?' I ask.

'What does all what mean?' asks Aren in reply.

'All this talk about the gift. What exactly does it have to do with me? Is that why Simon's following me? Is that why the cat came back to life?'

They look at me as though I'm speaking a foreign language. And I thought they knew everything. I seriously thought they were watching my every move and waiting for me to find my way to them. So I tell them what happened after they visited me in my room. How Simon lay in wait for me, how I found him on my doorstep the next day, and how since then he's been following me everywhere. And how the cat was dead and then alive again.

'All because of a kiss,' I say.

When I finally tell them that I was delirious and fell asleep outside in the snow on Evelin's steps, the two of them start to get nervous.

'No frostbite?' says Elia.

'Nothing,' I say. 'The cold saved me. I felt better outside than I did in the house. I thought I was on fire from the inside out.'

They look at each other. They simply look at each other. After a while I've had enough and I say, 'What's happening to me?'

'What *happened* to me, you mean,' says Elia.

'Whatever,' I say, waiting for him to continue. But it's Aren who says, 'From the moment you took the boy's gift, it wanted to live on inside you. It's like a parasite that can't survive without a host. That's why it made you swallow it. It liberated certain talents in you. That's why we became visible for you and that's why you received a power that apparently makes Simon obey you, and the thing with the cat . . .'

Aren falls silent and shakes his head.

'Tell her everything,' Elia tells him. 'We've kept it from her long enough.'

After a long pause Aren says, 'We don't know what's happening to you. There's a certain point when the gift tries to put down roots. The symptoms are severe fever – the feeling that your insides are burning. You're not the only one it's happened to. We can't take care of every dead child – we simply don't always get there on time. And besides, few gifts have the strength to find themselves a host. And even if they do find one, the host hardly ever survives. The fact that you could see us on the first day says something about the strength of the gift. And the fact that you're still alive says something about your strength and the luck you've had. That night the dead boy's gift fused firmly with your own. And the cold saved you, so—'

'Just a second,' I interrupt him. 'You mean I *could* have died?'

'Wrong,' answers Elia calmly. 'We were sure you would die.'

I look from one to the other. I see no movement in their faces, no emotion.

*'You pricks!'* I say loudly. *'You were going to let me die just like that?'*

Aren folds his arms. That gives me my answer. Elia says, 'Please, don't speak so loudly.'

'Why couldn't you tell me?' I ask quietly.

'Because we couldn't have helped you. It . . . it had to happen.'

'What good would it have done?' asks Aren. 'What good would it have done you to know you were about to die?'

I don't know. I have no idea.

'I don't trust you any more,' I say.

'We never asked you to trust us,' says Aren.

'But it's your fault that I've this crappy gift inside me.'

'Theoretically speaking,' says Elia.

'You said it yourself,' I remind him. 'You came too late, you messed up. Whatever you were supposed to do, you messed it up. You can't just leave me like this – you can't! What am I supposed to do now? I . . . I mean, isn't there a way of getting the gift out again?'

Aren shakes his head.

'You don't want that. It's far too dangerous, especially now that it's put down roots. Forget it. You don't want—'

'Of course I do!' I interrupt him. 'Do you think I want to run around resurrecting dead cats and turning people into slaves for the rest of my life?'

'No,' says Aren. 'I don't think you do, but I do think you don't realize what you might lose by rejecting it.'

'You're talking about my life again, aren't you?' I laugh. 'As if you care!'

'Not your life,' says Elia. 'Your own gift would disappear and leave you empty. You'd just be a girl with no talents. One girl among many. Do you want to risk that?'

*Do I?*

I try to imagine what that would mean. What kind of talents do I have?

'Many,' says Elia quietly.

'But I don't know what they are.'

'You'll learn what they are, believe me.'

At that moment a piece of wood in the fireplace crackles loudly. I look over and see sparks rising up from the flames. It's like a scene from a film. Suddenly the whole situation becomes clear for the very first time. I'm sitting here on a sofa that Evelin can't see, talking to two creatures, and I don't know if they really exist or who they are. Sitting and talking about my death and the loss of my talents.

'What do you have to do with all of this?'

When I ask this question, Aren gets up and goes over to the fireplace. He puts more wood on the fire and stands there with his back to us.

'He doesn't want us to talk about it,' Elia explains, 'even though he knows we owe you an explanation. Don't be angry with him – he just doesn't want to be part of it.'

'What about you?'

'I'll tell you because I want to. We should have told you earlier that you were in danger.'

He gestures briefly with his hand at the room around us.

'Everything you see here doesn't exist. At least not in your world. Imagine two circles that intersect. This is our circle. There are places that belong only to us. They don't exist for you. We move through your world, whereas our world remains invisible.'

'I worked that much out,' I say.

'How did you notice us?' asks Elia.

'I saw you. A couple of times on the street and once in the underground and then on the ice when a boy nearly drowned. A woman helped him. She climbed into the water naked and helped him out of the hole. I also saw how you change shape. Why do you do that?'

Elia looks around briefly and bends forward as though trying to prevent the others from hearing him.

'We're here to protect you,' he says. 'As soon as you call for us, we come. We're also here to ease your death. When a child dies we take its gift and plant it. We plant it in the ground and let it put down roots. That's why we're here.'

'Are you guardian angels?'

Elia shakes his head.

'We don't have a name. We go to any child who believes in us and calls us, no matter what name they call us by. In death nearly every child calls for us. But it's often too late and we can't help any more.'

'And the boy in the coffin . . .'

'. . . didn't have a chance to call for anybody. It was an accident. He died and we came too late. You know the rest.'

Yes, I know the rest. Alissa falling through the snow. Alissa landing in a crypt. Alissa and a child's coffin with metal fastenings.

'Where do you come from?'

'That's none of your business,' replies Elia.

'What?'

'I said it's none of your business. We just *are*. I won't tell you any more than that because you don't need to know any more than that.'

He falls silent. I wait, but nothing else comes. I can't believe it.

'What do you mean? That's it? That's everything?'

'That's everything.'

'Great! Thank you very much. And what do I do now?' I keep asking. I can hear my voice growing louder. 'What happens now? What do I do with this wretched gift?'

Elia looks over to Aren, who turns around as though on cue and comes back over to us.

'You can't tell her, can you?' he says.

Elia looks down at his hands again. Aren presses his lips together.

'What can't he tell me?' I ask.

'That we won't help you. That it's not up to us to interfere in your life. We have to let you go. You can't come back here any more.'

My mouth drops. Even though I'm shocked, I'm still quite calm. I have the strange feeling that I mustn't move too quickly, almost as though sudden movements will make everything around me disappear. I put the cup of tea down carefully and get up.

'And suppose I want to get rid of my gift?' I ask. 'Suppose I don't care about my talents?'

'Then there's nothing to be done,' says Aren. 'We won't get involved.'

'What . . . ? But you can't just . . .'

'We won't do it.'

I try to talk calmly, but the words hurtle out of me. 'You've been playing with me. You asked me if I wanted to risk giving away my gift but you never intended to help me!'

They look at me. They don't deny it.

*'And what do I do now with this wretched gift?'* I cry out, punching my fist into my stomach so that it hurts. *'What on earth do I do with it?'*

'Shall I be honest?' asks Aren. The distance has returned to his gaze and his eyes are a thousand miles away.

'Out with it,' I say.

'It's your problem,' he replies. 'The best thing you can do is learn to live with it.'

*My problem.*

I look at them. Aren. Elia.

*My problem.*

I feel my knees shaking. Cautiously I sit back down on the sofa.

*What did I expect?* I ask myself.

Not only that they would help me. That would be a lie.

*What on earth did I expect?*

The answer comes quietly.

*You dreamed of angels, Alissa. You dreamed of becoming one of them. You thought that you'd give anything for the chance of turning into a raven. To be able to fly, to be a miracle worker. Anything at all. Because maybe as an angel you could visit the dead. Then you could see your father again and so many things would be possible. Anything at all. Anything at all.*

'I thought . . .' I stammer and fall silent.

'This is no place for you,' says Aren. I'm sure he knows

261

exactly what I dreamed up for myself. 'We're not like each other. We're not here because we enjoy it, do you understand that? If it was up to me you would never have been able to find this place. But that's another issue altogether. I hope we've understood each other. Be happy that the gift didn't kill you. Be grateful for your life and make the best of it. Learn to live with your power and find out what it is.'

He pauses so that the words hit home.

'Elia will accompany you out now. And please don't be so stupid as to think you're welcome here just because you can see our world. A lot of people have been locked away because they see us and can't talk about anything else. Make yourself understand that your world has no interest in people like you. I say that for your own good. Learn to live with the gift.'

With these words he turns away and leaves the room. Elia gets up too and offers me his hand.

'Come.'

'I'm afraid,' I say, and remain sitting. 'Can we . . . I mean, can't we talk a little longer?'

'Your friend's waiting.'

'Just a few more minutes, please, I . . .'

Suddenly I start to cry. It's as though a balloon has burst. The tears pour out of me and I bury my face in my hands.

'I . . . I don't want any of this. How . . .'

I touch my lips.

'. . . how I am supposed to control it? I mean . . . I can't kiss anybody ever again without turning them into my slave straight away. What is it? What does this gift do? What . . .'

'You have to find out for yourself what it means and where your talents will lead you. Learn to understand the gift.'

'But what is there to understand? Simon's following me and I'm afraid of him. He . . . he says he belongs to me. He wants . . . he says he can see you as well . . . Why can he see you? Why . . .'

'He can see us?'

I nod and wipe the tears out of my eyes.

'Alissa?'

I didn't notice the movement. Elia was standing a metre away and suddenly he's speaking into my ear. One of his hands is on my arm, the other one gently touches the back of my head. I can feel the calm radiating from him.

'If the gift is what it appears to be,' he says, 'then you have to be very careful with yourself. Do you understand?'

'OK,' I say, sniffing. 'But what . . . what is it?'

'It's strong and very rare. It has become a gate. Take care of it and think carefully about who you let through.'

'What? What are you talking about?'

Elia smiles.

'I'm talking about you,' he says.

'About me?'

'About you, and now . . .'

He lets go of me.

'. . . it's time for you to go.'

He waits, I wait, then suddenly it bursts out of me. The calm has gone. In an instant my confusion has turned into anger, as though somebody has flipped a switch. I feel like slapping Elia's face.

'Oh God!'

I kick against the table, the cup falls on to the carpet, a tea stain begins to spread. I'm on my feet and get so close to Elia that he pulls his head back in surprise.

'You don't want to help me!' I hiss at him.

'Correct. I can't. It—'

'You *can't* help me?' I interrupt him. 'What does that mean? You're standing there talking about some mystical shit that I can't get my head around, but really you only want to tell me that you *can't* help me. Have I understood you correctly?'

He looks at me. I turn around and shout out loud into the room, 'Can any of you in here do anything?'

An unpleasant quiet spreads. Nobody is reading any more, all conversations have faded, they are all looking at me.

'Alissa?'

Elia plucks at my arm.

'Please, Alissa, let's—'

'Take her out,' interrupts a woman from the next table. Her voice is cool and sober. She has no intention of arguing with me, she has no intention of answering my questions. She simply wants me to leave. Quickly.

'Thank you very much,' I say quietly, grabbing my coat. 'I'll find the exit by myself. Thank you very, very much.'

I'm an angry child and stomp through the room without looking at anybody. I leave the double doors open behind me and march down the stairs and through the entrance hall out into the night, which in that brief period of time has turned into a grey morning. I can feel the cry of anger that has built up inside me. But I won't shout. I'll stand here calmly until all the anger has wandered down through my feet and into the ground.

'Everything OK?'

I jump. I didn't see her. Evelin is sitting over to the left on the top step. She's tucked her hands under her armpits. I look depressed and worn out, but Evelin looks like somebody who's just heard some very bad news.

'I'm fine,' I lie. 'But what's the matter with you?'

'We're in trouble,' says Evelin, getting up. She shakes her gloves free of snow and puts them on. Her gaze moves past me to the villa. I turn around and see the door falling silently shut.

'Simon's on his way,' she says.

## Simon The Loving One

'Technology. Works wonders.'

'What?'

'Communication. Everything is so much faster. You can throw somebody to the ground at the speed of light and they wake up at the speed of light.'

She's silent. I can hear her breathing.

'Nervous?' I ask.

'Simon?' she says finally.

'Wow! I thought you'd recognize my voice straight away. I'm rather disappointed.'

Silence again.

'Did I frighten you, Evelin? How does it feel to knock Simon out on the ice and then the phone rings and good old Simon's on the other end?'

'Not good,' she says.

'That's what I thought. Do you know who I'm looking for?'

'Let me guess.'

'Go ahead, guess,' I say, but she doesn't say anything and

I keep talking. 'You think you're tough, eh? You think you're really hard. Well, you can think what you like, but I've got a few surprises for you. You and I aren't finished with each other yet. And don't even think about hanging up. There are a couple of people here who wouldn't find that one bit funny. How about a little background music?'

I hold the receiver up in the air and say, 'All right, old folks, how about a hello for the lady?'

*'Don't tell him anything, Evelin!'* Leon cries.

'Hello,' I say into the receiver, 'it's me again. I would have liked to give you a live performance by Grandma Netta, but the old lady fainted on the spot. I didn't know she was so frail. Or do you think I'm a good enough reason for people to faint?'

Silence.

'I'll take that as a *no*. And now put Alissa on the phone.'

'She's not here.'

This is all getting a bit much. I feel as though the back of my skull has a hole in it. I have to go outside into the cold. The cold will heal me.

'I'll give you one minute,' I say, 'then I'll start thinking about how to make old people cross the pain barrier without getting my hands dirty.'

'You'd never—'

'I'd do anything to find Alissa,' I interrupt. I mean it too. My body's crying out for her. It's like an addiction. Wrong – it *is* an addiction. I can feel her under my skin. My every breath strives in her direction. Alissa.

'How do you think I know,' I continue, 'that you're running around like a bodyguard with Leon's mobile phone, so you can be reached in an emergency?'

Silence.

'Do you think Leon told me just like that? Evelin, wake up. I know you're hiding her from me and that's ridiculous, because she belongs to me and nothing can keep us from being together. I'll do everything in my power to make that happen, do you understand? You can forget your minute now – time's up. Give me the right answers or I'll lose it, OK?'

'OK.'

'Where is she?'

'Behind me, in a villa.'

'Fetch her.'

'I'm not going in there. She . . . she's talking to some people.'

'What kind of people?'

'Friends of hers.'

'Alissa doesn't have any friends that I don't know.'

'Things have changed since you dumped her.'

'Bullshit! Where are you?'

'I don't know.'

'Evelin . . .'

'I really don't know! We sailed down the Havel in the canoe and I fell asleep on the way. We could be anywhere.'

'Look around. What can you see?'

'A pathway . . . I'm sitting in front of a villa.'

'Go to the road.'

'There isn't any—'

'Go to the road. Where do you think you are? This isn't Scandinavia. Every house in this city is next to a road, so don't treat me like an idiot.'

I have to gasp for air. I didn't notice that I was shouting at her.

'Go on,' I say in a friendly tone of voice.

For a while I can only hear her steps. I press the receiver firmly to my ear. I want to know if she's talking to Alissa. A villa and friends? Has Alissa found them? If Alissa has found them, then . . .'

Evelin's back.

'The road's called *Wannseebadweg.*'

'Give me the house number.'

'The villa hasn't got a number, it's just a ruin.'

'Look around. Give me something.'

'There's a post box a few metres away.'

'Excellent. Good girl. Do you know what you're going to do now? You're going to stand next to the road and wait for your friend. And when your friend comes out of the villa, both of you are going to stand at the side of the road and wait for me. Nice Simon is coming to collect the love of his life. Do you think that's soppy? You don't know the meaning of the word. You've got no idea what love is. I could weep with love.'

I dry my eyes. I'm actually crying.

'And believe me, if I turn up and you're not there, then I'll take care of these two old people. I'm capable of anything, OK? Do you understand?'

'I understand.'

'Good. See you soon,' I say and hang up.

# Evelin The Best Friend

Alissa blinks, confused.

'You did what?' she repeats.

'I had to tell him. He threatened your grandparents! I mean, what was I supposed to do?'

'You could have lied.'

'Ever tried lying in a situation like that?'

Alissa looks at me strangely. I don't understand anything any more. Isn't she worried about Leon and Grandma Netta?

'Let's go,' she says.

'Alissa, I—'

'If Simon finds the villa,' she interrupts, 'then he'll understand the connection. He'll be able to see them. He'll know who they are. Is that what you want?'

She looks at the villa and repeats quietly, 'Is that what you want?'

I don't answer. I really couldn't care less whether Simon finds the villa or not. There was a moment when I sensed that something was there, just before I left the room with the fireplace. I could feel the presence of others and for a moment I thought I could see the room's splendour out of the corner of my eye. But asking me to worry about it is a bit too much. For me this world remains unreal. So I respond neutrally to Alissa's question. She immediately interprets this the wrong way.

'Come on, Evelin! It's about time you started to think. We need a taxi, then we'll worry about Grandma Netta and Leon. But first we need to get out of here. And then . . .'

She smiles at me.

'. . . we'll deal with Simon.'

The way she says it scares me. I'm scared for Simon.


We walk down *Wannseebadweg*. Fir trees to our left and right, the grey blue morning over us, Alissa always one step ahead.

'What happened in there?' I want to know.

'Later,' she says.

'And why can Simon see them as well? How long have you known that?'

'He told me before on the ice, but that doesn't matter now, they don't want anything to do with me. It's over.'

'Oh.'

I try to keep up and put my arm through hers. Alissa shakes off my arm and turns around angrily.

'*Oh*? Is that all you can think of to say? A crappy little *oh*? I expected something better from you.'

'I'm sorry, but—'

'I'm not enough for them. I'm not one of them, do you understand? I'm just Alissa and that's not enough. And it would have been so beautiful. I . . . I would have been like an angel, you know. I could have helped. I . . . I would have looked after you. I might have . . . I might have found out something about my father. Who knows? But they don't want me. They want me to forget about them. Does that make any sense to you?'

'Not one bit,' I say.

I'm sorry.'

Suddenly she hugs me.

'I'm sorry. I didn't want to shout at you. I'm really sorry.'

We stand on the street, Alissa crying and me holding her in my arms. Helpless.

'Everything'll be OK,' I say flatly. What a cliché!

She sniffs.

'Maybe it's better this way,' she says.

'Maybe.'

She tells me what a gift is, how it develops and dies with age if it's not taken care of properly. As I listen, I ask myself what this means for me. What's my gift? What kind of talents are hidden in me and what kind of person will I become?

'The boy's gift,' says Alissa, 'joined with my gift and all of this chaos was the result. Elia called me a gate. I don't get it, do you? I . . . I've got a devoted kitten and a guy stalking me. What's that got to do with a gate? I make people dependent on me. What kind of crappy talent is that?'

We see a brightly lit petrol station through the dense trees.

'Do you think Simon's done something to them?' she asks.

'It didn't sound like it. Leon called out in the background and told me I should keep my mouth—'

I don't get any further. Headlights cut through the darkness like lasers and fall on us so that we automatically throw up our arms to shield our eyes. An engine revs up and a car shoots towards us along with the light.

For one stupid second I expect the driver to dip his lights and slow down because he's seen us. Until it clicks. A real clicking sound like you never expect to hear. I hear it. Then Alissa pulls at my arm and we run to the left into the woods.

# Simon The Loving One

I'm driving down *Havelchaussee*, alongside the river. My old man's wheels probably haven't been fired up like this since they were built. My old man drives as though a child's about to sprout out of the asphalt at any minute. If that happens I'll run it over, put the car in reverse and run it over again.

I'm satisfied. Leon and Grandma Netta are locked up in their bedroom, Evelin's standing at the edge of the street, waiting for me to arrive, but what the fuck is Alissa doing?

I turn on the fog lights. The map's on the passenger seat. I'll be there in another quarter of an hour or so.

A glance in the rearview mirror.

I know I won't meet any cops. I'm immune to all external forces. I'm driving to my loved one.

When I reach the *Avus*, the feeling grabs me. The map doesn't make any sense any more because a magnet has kicked in. If you were to put a blindfold on me now or chop off my legs, I'd still find Alissa. Always. My compass is fixed on her. I roll down the window and stick out my head. The wind hits my face, the cold rushes into my mouth and fills me up. I press the accelerator all the way down and rev the engine up to a hundred and twenty.

Woods on the right, motorway on the left, the illuminated street in front of me and no traffic. A petrol station. I turn right at the petrol station and then I see them. In front of me. Like trapped deer. Deer in coats and woolly hats. Two thin lines on the asphalt. I blink and they disappear. To the right. Into the woods.

No problem.

It's like one of the *Star Wars* films, only I'm driving my old man's wheels instead of a nifty speeder bike. But I'm on the right track and the trees aren't too dense. I'll get through.

*Over there!*

Apart from the engine the only noise is the scraping of tree trunks as they peel the paint off my car, then the horrible crunching of the frame as I speed over roots and holes. Snow powders up around me as if I'm driving through a desert. Snow falls from the trees and the flailing branches. But I'm on the right track and I can see Alissa and Evelin ducking behind trees, running. I see everything. And I speed up.

# Alissa *The Winter Child*

The car rumbles loudly after us as if it means to flatten the trees around us. I run in front of Evelin, her heavy breathing a threatening presence in my back. I turn around and glance behind me. The car's progress is slow, it grazes against trees, rolls over bushes and bounces around on the uneven ground as though it were made of rubber. The headlights stab bright lances into the grey morning like a strobe light on overdrive.

Evelin catches up. We run across a clearing and find a second woodland path.

'. . . better not . . .'

'. . . it's . . .'

'. . . I know . . .'

'. . . but . . .'

'. . . come . . .'

I pull her further into the thick woodland. We'll give Simon a run for his money! Hurriedly I push her in front of me and then the ground disappears under my left foot and pain shoots up my leg.

'Shit!'

I pull my leg out of the hole. It's like a repeat of Christmas Day night, only this time I haven't fallen through the snow. I'm just stuck. But that's enough.

'Alissa . . . ?'

Evelin helps me up. I stagger and cry out. I can't put any weight on my foot and I fall into the snow.

'Get out of here!' I say.

'Never.'

'Please, Evelin.'

'I won't get out of here. I—'

Her shadow falls over me. The car has appeared behind her, the headlights bathing her in a harsh glare. The roar of the engine seems to be the only noise in the world.

Evelin turns around, takes three steps forward, and I see her shrug her shoulders.

'No!' I cry out to her.

But she doesn't hear.

# Evelin The Best Friend

If it was up to me, we'd run down the woodland path. But that would mean making things easier for Simon. *If it is Simon,* I think. I'd laugh if I had enough breath. Nobody else would think of hunting Alissa and me through a snowy wood at dawn, not caring whether he drives his car into the ground in the process. Nobody else apart from Simon would be capable of it.

'Shit!'

I turn around, a stitch in my side, sweat in my eyes, legs like lead. Alissa has fallen through a hole in the snow up to her knee. By the time I reach her side, she's managed to pull herself out. I help her up, she tries to put weight on her foot and cries out. Before I can catch her, she's lying in the snow and saying to me, 'Get out of here.'

'Never,' I say, trying to help her up.

'Please, Evelin.'

'I won't get out of here, I—'

The landscape around me flares up in its whiteness. The

trees become paper cut-outs, the engine roars as though an enormous animal is sprinting towards us. I don't know where the feeling suddenly comes from, but my fear has gone and left anger in its place. My hands form fists. I feel as though my entire body has switched on to automatic. My shoulders, my arms, my breath, my gaze. I am living anger.

'I've had enough of this,' I say, turning and walking towards the car.

It's a strange moment, because I know that nothing will happen to me. It's a good feeling. I know that I'm in control of the situation. It's like standing on the ten-metre diving board and not being able to go back. Sticking your nose into something and then suddenly everybody is looking at you. Sharing a first kiss with somebody. And being aware – being completely aware.

'No!' cries Alissa behind me.

But I don't hear.

# 41

# Simon The Loving One

*That cow! Who does that little lesbian think she is? What is she thinking? What on earth?*

I step on the brake, the wheels lock and the rear of the car swings out.

*How dare she! What does she think I'm doing here? She must be tired of living.*

I move in slow motion. My mouth's open, my fingers gripping the steering wheel which dances and vibrates under my hands. Tree trunks move slowly past, branches crack, then the spinning gets faster and faster and there's a dull crash and I think, *That was it.*

But that wasn't it at all. The spinning gets worse and then comes the impact. I feel it on all sides, I'm flung around. The door flies open, my mouth screams and I feel as though my insides are being spun out of me.

# Alissa The Winter Child

Evelin spreads out her arms as if to embrace the car. She stands there and . . . isn't afraid. That's exactly how she stands there.

Then suddenly the car starts to spin. The beams from the headlights pierce the woodland and dazzle me. For one second I can see Simon's contorted face behind the steering wheel, mouth open, eyes wide. The car approaches Evelin like a spinning top that's lost its balance. She doesn't move an inch. Arms wide open, shoulders up, fearless and angry.

# Evelin The Best Friend

I know. I'll stop him. I know for certain that the car will come to a halt right in front of me. And then I'll take care of Simon. Then I'll finish him. I know.

*Yes!*

I've never felt like this before. Even though I'm blinded by the headlights, the strangest pictures pass in front of my eyes. I see Nina coming towards me and hugging me. I see my father opening the fridge, asking if I'm hungry. My mother calls to me from a window, *Evelin, are you coming?*

And I've never felt like this before. So certain. Never.

I smile.

And then the moment has passed.

# 44

What remains is the ticking of the engine and the silence of a winter's morning. A thick curtain of snow sinks into the quiet. It meanders past the branches of the fir trees and begins to cover the scenery with a fine layer of powder.

The winter child kneels forward on the ground. She is holding the best friend in her arms. The loving one is lying half in and half out of the car. His face is bloody, his mouth open and silent. The engine ticks, a branch breaks, then two ravens land on an uprooted tree trunk.

The winter child doesn't look up. She can see the sequence of pictures – the bonnet of the car hitting the best friend like a whale's tail, driving her into a fir tree. The car coming to a standstill a couple of metres away. Then silence.

'. . . please . . .'

The winter child strokes the best friend's face. She rocks her as though she's holding a child in her arms. The best friend's face is white. A single drop of blood has trickled out of the corner of her mouth and run down her chin. The best friend's eyes are open a crack, but no matter how the winter child tries, she cannot see anything in the lifeless pupils.

'Please, Evelin . . . it was . . . why did you . . . why . . . ?'

The winter child wrinkles her nose. There's a scream inside her that has been there for a long time. And as the winter child raises her head and looks up into the dawn sky, she opens her mouth and screams her desperation out into the day.

Only the snowflakes answer her.

The two ravens on the tree trunk do not stir.

The winter child looks at them and says, 'Get out of here!'

The ravens spread their wings and leave.

Snow covers the car and the loving one, snow covers the winter child and the best friend. The ticking of the engine has long since ceased. The only sound is the winter child's voice. She is talking to the best friend. Later she won't remember a single word. It will be as though she never spoke.

Eventually all words are used up. The winter child falls silent and moves close to the best friend's face. Their lips touch and the winter child blows her breath into the best friend's mouth. The kiss is long and loving. When the winter child raises her head again, she smiles.

'Evelin,' she says quietly, brushing a strand of hair back behind the best friend's ear. 'Evelin!'

# 45

# Alissa The Winter Child

I feel numb when I look at Simon. He's hanging half in and half out of the car. His mouth is open, his eyes closed. I know he's dead. There's a frozen pool of blood behind his head, his left hand is lying open in the snow as though waiting for something. I take his hand. It's stiff. I stroke his fingers in farewell and bend over his ear.

'I'm sorry,' I say and leave him alone.

I think it's only when the fire engines and ambulances arrive that reality sets in. As if my consciousness is a layer of ice that can only bear a certain weight. With the arrival of other people reality becomes too heavy and the ice gives way.

I start to cry. I begin to thrash around when one of the ambulance crew puts a blanket around me. Then I calm down again. I'm asked questions, I'm given tea to drink, but I can't swallow any of it. My teeth chatter against the mug and I spill half the contents.

They carry Simon's body into the ambulance. First they

have to lay him out straight. Somebody has closed his mouth. His left hand still looks as though it's waiting for something.

*I couldn't give it to you,* I think, closing my eyes tight until I see flashes.

*Wrong. I didn't want to.*

'Everything OK?'

I murmur a *yes* and look over at Evelin. The ambulance man tells me I don't have to look but I shake my head. I want him to leave me alone.

They have fewer problems with Evelin. I've laid her out on the snow and put my coat under her head. I'm sitting on the bonnet of an ambulance wearing only a jumper and I don't feel any cold. I'm the winter child. The cold is my home.

They lift Evelin up and put her on the stretcher. She looks like an Egyptian queen. Her hair is hanging out of her woolly hat and I wish I could tuck it behind her ears.

I sit next to her in the ambulance and hold her hand.

Mum and Robert suddenly appear. And Evelin's parents. They cry and look at me, then Evelin's mother folds me in her arms. I can hear her voice and I don't understand a single word. I wish Evelin could be here to explain what it means. I'm on completely the wrong wavelength.

And the whole time the lights from the ambulance colour the grey morning. They glide over tree trunks, brushing over the snow and people's shocked faces. The gliding colours remind me of fish underwater, a silent world that has no beginning and no end. I want to be part of it, I want to look shocked and be afraid. I'm not afraid. I'm not a part of this world.

# Part VI

# Robert The Stepfather

We try hot milk and honey. We give her sleeping tablets and wait for her to get tired. It's no use. After an hour Sarah's eyes start to close. She kisses Alissa on the head and tells her that she loves her. After that we're alone.

'You can go to bed too if you want,' Alissa says to me.

'I'm not tired.'

'You're a liar.'

I shrug my shoulders apologetically and don't know what else to say.

Alissa seems so normal. We drove by to see Grandma Netta and Leon on the way back. The front door wasn't closed properly. Simon had locked the two of them in the bedroom. Alissa comforted her grandma. Where does she find the strength?

'I don't know what the matter is,' I say, honestly.

Shock seems to be the wrong word. If Alissa's in shock, then I'm blind to it. Maybe it'll come later. Maybe she needs to sleep first and wake up. If only she would sleep!

'You think I'm not sad enough,' she says.

I don't answer her. Her best friend is dead. How am I supposed to reply?

'I am sad,' says Alissa, 'for Simon.'

'And for Evelin,' she adds after a couple of seconds, closing her eyes. When the first tears come, I lean forward and press her close to me and think that she probably is in shock. Delayed shock.

'Go to sleep now,' I say, kissing her on the cheek.

Alissa looks at me, her eyes bright behind their film of tears.

'Goodnight,' she says.

'Goodnight.'

I leave the room and stand in the hallway. Later I might think of better questions. I don't know what I expect. When I saw Alissa holding her dead friend's hand in the ambulance, for a moment I felt as though I was watching the wrong scene. Only when Sarah and I went closer and Alissa noticed us did the scene turn into what it really was – a person grieving for another person. What exactly it was before then, I can't say.

I'd really like to go back in there and ask her about it, but then I hear her voice through the door and reconsider. Everyone has their own way of dealing with what they've gone through. Even Sarah talked to herself in the months following her husband's death. It's time for me to go to bed.

I creep quietly through the hallway into the living room

where I go out on to the balcony and smoke a last cigarette. My thoughts are going round in circles. I'm trying to understand things that make no sense. After I've extinguished the cigarette in the snow, I go into the bathroom and brush my teeth. I turn off all the lights and lie down in bed next to Sarah. I cuddle up to her back and we lie there like that without saying a word.

'It's like a curse,' says Sarah finally.

I don't answer. I know what she's talking about. Death is a shadow that has settled over her life and doesn't want to go away again. I keep my mouth shut. Any reaction would be the wrong one. Instead I look out of the window. Outside the morning is grey and heavy. It's half past six. Soon the door will open and Jan will ask if we're still alive or never want to have breakfast again. He'll say it exactly like that – *Are you still alive or are we never having breakfast again?* And I'll reply that of course we're still alive. And then I'll get up and make breakfast, same as always.

# Alissa The Winter Child

'I am sad,' I say, 'for Simon.'

Robert nods, rubbing his face.

'And for Evelin,' I add, closing my eyes.

I know that this is exactly the reaction Robert expects. Before he spends the entire morning by my bedside, I'd rather give him what he wants to hear. I'm surprised how easy it is to cry. I almost burst out laughing. The corners of my mouth are twitching.

'Go to sleep now,' says Robert, kissing me on the cheek.

*There's no need to be sad*, I want to tell him, but I can't. He would never understand.

'Goodnight,' I say.

'Goodnight.'

He leaves my room and closes the door behind him. I look over to the left and smile at Evelin.

'Was I too theatrical?'

'You were OK,' she says. 'I don't know what you had to do to squeeze out those tears. You'd never have fooled me.'

'I *am* sad,' I say.

'But not because of me,' says Evelin.

'No, not because of you,' I agree.

It's the first time we've talked to each other. On the journey to the hospital she came to me, held my hand the whole time, kissed my cheek and was so close to me that I wanted to tell her parents that Evelin hadn't gone, she was here holding my hand.

*Look!*

Now she's sitting on the chair next to my bed, looking the way she did two hours ago. The blood has vanished from her face. I ask myself if she'll always wear those clothes.

'Of course not,' she says.

'Not that they don't suit you,' I say.

She laughs. She's laughing at me because she knows exactly why I'm sad. I'd like to be in her position. I wish we could swap places.

'You don't really mean that,' she says, turning serious again.

'I should have thought of it the very moment Elia told me I was a gate.'

'No, you shouldn't,' says Evelin.

'I should have. I always thought this was all about me – Simon following me, the kitten following me. When really all Simon wanted was to become one of them. Even though he didn't know what that meant, it drew him in. When Elia told me I should think about who I let through, I should have realized.'

Evelin shrugs her shoulders.

'He didn't tell you the only catch is that you have to be dead to become one of them, did he?'

'You're right, but . . .'

I realize that I'm looking for an explanation that could have prevented all this. And I'm also looking for an excuse.

'You know, all the time I really didn't care what happened to Simon, I just wanted to be one of them. Nothing else mattered. It's so horribly ironic that it happened to you.'

'That was chance.'

'But maybe that's how they come into being,' I say. 'By chance.'

'I don't think so, but who knows?'

Evelin puts her hands on mine.

'Don't look so tragic. Guilt doesn't suit you. Whatever your kiss triggered off in Simon, he bore the same responsibility as you. We all messed up something. If only I'd told you there was no kitten, if only I'd led you to the spot where I'd buried it, who knows how things might have turned out then?'

We both look towards the end of the bed at the same time. It's reassuring to understand it all now. The kitten belongs to them. It's lying between my feet. It was all a stupid mistake. And I seriously thought I could bring back the dead.

'I thought I could bring back the dead,' I say. What I don't tell her is that I thought I could find a way of reaching my father. *If I had been one of those beings, what could have stopped me? What could have stopped me from bringing my father back into this life?*

I know that's stupid. I envy the abilities my best friend has now, but losing her tears me apart.

'I'm stupid,' I say, shaking my head.

'No, you're a dreamer,' says Evelin.

I look at her. My voice is quiet as I speak.

'Was it very bad?'

Evelin merely looks at me. I lean out of bed and brush her hair behind her ears. I'll really miss touching her.

'Will you help me?' I ask.

'I promised you that on the journey here, Alissa, so let's drop the rhetorical questions, OK? I'll help you if you're sure you won't regret it.'

'I'm sure.'

'It's risky. Elia and Aren wouldn't do it out of respect for the gift and because they were afraid of hurting you.'

'I know, but if you—'

'I'm not afraid of hurting you. And don't start on me with respect.'

I can't see any movement in her face as she says it. No emotion. Evelin is pure and clear.

'Thank you,' I say.

'Now?' she asks.

I want to say *No*.

'You can say *No*,' says Evelin.

'Now,' I say, making my voice sound certain.

Evelin pushes down the bed covers, pulls up my T-shirt and

places her hand between my breasts. Slowly her hand wanders down and comes to rest above my bellybutton.

'If it doesn't work,' I say nervously, 'it doesn't matter. I—'

'Don't be afraid,' says Evelin, and her hand disappears inside me.

A limp feeling spreads throughout my body, as though I've been lifted up by my hands and feet. Evelin has closed her eyes and her hand has disappeared inside me up to the wrist. I can't tell where the entry point lies. Her arm looks as though it's growing out of my stomach.

'Yes,' says Evelin, taking out her hand again.

I look down at my stomach. The skin looks as it did before. It isn't even red. I blink confusedly. The floating feeling has disappeared.

'Can I see it?' I ask.

Evelin opens her hand. The gift is a purple plant the size of a thumb. It lies hard and shiny on Evelin's palm. It has delicate roots and fine hairs on the stem and leaves.

'And what happens now?' I ask. 'Is everything . . .'

'Everything's fine now,' says Evelin, closing her hand.

I try to smile when I realize what she's saying. I want to be brave. I want to cry.

'You're going now,' I say.

Evelin nods.

'And you're not coming back.'

'Of course I'm coming back. But you won't see me any more — that's over now.'

And as she says it, I feel the heat crawling out of every corner of my room. I feel as though I'm attracting it – heat from the radiators, heat from the candles, heat from everywhere. It collects in me and wanders through my body up to my head until my head feels like a hot air balloon. Tears shoot into my eyes, real hot tears, and I know I've never felt as sad as I do at this moment. I feel as though it's a thousand times worse than the death of my father. It's . . .

'That's the pain,' says Evelin, stroking my face. 'Your gift is gone. That's the pain that comes afterwards, Alissa. Calm down.'

But I know it's more, I know. I hear myself sob. I don't want Evelin to go. I don't want it to be over. I want to see her again. Day after day. I've made a mistake. I've lost my best friend. I . . .

'I don't want you to go,' I say, wrinkling my nose.

Evelin smiles tiredly and answers, 'Say, *So long, Evelin*.'

'So long, Evelin,' I say quietly.

My best friend leans forward and kisses me on the mouth. I want to keep hold of her kiss, I want to burn the feeling of her lips into my memory, but the kiss is already over and Evelin has stood up and says in farewell:

# Evelin The Best Friend

'I don't want you to be afraid, Alissa. You know as soon as you call me, I'll be close by. I'll look after you, do you hear? And don't worry about your gift.'

I press the hand holding her gift to my chest.

'I'll plant it for you and it will flourish, do you understand?'

Alissa nods.

'There's really no reason to be afraid,' I repeat. 'Nothing will separate us.'

'And when I die?' asks Alissa quietly.

'You won't die that quickly.'

'But when I die one day?'

'Then I'll be at your side.'

'Even when I'm grown up?'

'Even then, stupid.'

With these words I turn around and open the window. I know I'm just a ghostly figure for Alissa. In a few seconds I will have vanished. I swing myself up on to the window ledge. It's a movement that seems as familiar to me as if I've practised it my entire life. That's merely an illusion, of course. My life is barely two hours old.

For a few seconds I crouch on the ledge and look down at the street. I don't know what will happen next. And then when it happens I'm so surprised, I let out a loud cry. At the same moment my wings spread and I push myself off from the ledge. The wind seizes and lifts me and I glide on it over the city, motionless and quiet, until gravity demands that I beat my wings for the first time.

THE END

my thanks go to


micha & gregor
my two soul brothers
who stand by me
& my work


&


corinna
who heard the novel
in wind & rain
in an irish house


&


chantal
who found my novel
amongst
thousands of novels
& decided to
translate it